KITTY TAYLOR

By Sarah Colliver

I have always been interested in the female agents who were dropped into occupied France by the S.O.E. It is difficult to imagine how they must have felt, and the extremities which they endured, but I do know they were courageous. This story is fictional, with elements of reality. For example: 64 Baker Street – headquarters of the Special Operations Executive- is a real place. For the book to flow as a story, some elements & processes have been condensed, and I suggest if you would like to find out more about the real agents, there is plenty of material out there. You could begin with Violette Szabo, Noor Inayat Khan, and Virgina Hall. Although I have taken inspiration from the many stories I have read, Kitty and her life, is completely fictional, as are her family and everyone she encounters.

This is a complete work of fiction.

All rights reserved.

Sarah Colliver 2025

Sarah Colliver is a writer from the Forest of Dean, where she lives with her husband and tiny pug. This is her fifth book, second in the historical fiction genre. She loves writing fast-paced & immersive fiction stories, which are easy to devour and full of twists.

If you want to find out more about her, you will find her on Facebook, Instagram and Amazon.

I hope you enjoy Kitty's story ♥
much love
Sarah xx

Other books by this author:

WHEN WAR CAME TO LAUNDRY COTTAGE – a story of love, injustice and courage, set against the backdrop of the Homefront in WW2.

"Really enjoyed this book, it had me captivated from the start and I couldn't put it down. I loved the plot twist and so well written it kept me engaged throughout!"

IN DEEP – A spicy dramatic tale of danger in the mountains of Spain.

"I took this book on holiday and it was the perfect read for lying by the pool! The story grips you from the first chapter and having two-character perspectives makes it even better. I can't wait to read the second book to find out what happens next!"

DEEPER STILL – Sequel to In Deep – a gritty tale of revenge and new beginnings.

"Could not put this book down. A brilliant sequel to an equally good book 'In Deep.' Would highly recommend them both."

WE CLOSE OUR EYES – A fresh start, dark secrets, and dysfunctional marriage, set in the beautiful English countryside.

"I really enjoyed this story. I liked that the main character did not turn out as expected and the settings felt familiar and believable. I couldn't wait to finish the book to find out what happened but then was left wanting more. If you like psychological thrillers you will enjoy this gripping tale."

For my sister Janet, who is never forgotten.

We often learn too late, and our words must then be uttered into the ether, in the hope they find their way to the loved one already lost.

I hope you hear my words. x

KITTY TAYLOR by Sarah Colliver

Kitty needn't have worried if her courage would fail when the time came, because one hard shove from her companion, ensured there was no backing out. She plunged towards the earth grappling for her cord, as she fought the urge to scream. Somewhere beneath lay her destiny, and her immediate fate. Could she make it to the ground without being spotted by the enemy? Would she be captured or instantly executed by a machine gun? Were her comrades ensuring her safety already? Questions sped through her mind as fast as she hurtled towards the earth. She yanked the parachute cord and her descent slowed. A fusion of emotions flooded her, fear, exhilaration, excitement, and pain. It was more uncomfortable this time than the practice jump she completed back in the safety of home. Probably due to the wads of bank notes strapped to her body, and extra clothing she had on. There would be no denying what her purpose was if she were to be captured on landing, and there would be no time to reach for her cyanide capsule. Fear threatened to take hold, but she shook it away, she needed her wits about her if she was going to survive the next few weeks.

KITTY TAYLOR by Sarah Colliver

The beacons of her landing party grew nearer. She steered herself as best as she could towards them, praying it was not a trap. Her jumbled mind fought to remember the drill for landing; the last thing she needed was an injury. From this moment she was French to the core and fear she may slip up popped into her muddled thoughts, but she ushered it away, that wasn't an option. This was it; she was back, determined to do her bit for the war effort, where she knew her future lay, where she had always left her heart.

KITTY TAYLOR by Sarah Colliver

BEFORE, JUST A WAITRESS

Kitty adored her job in the Café de Flore and never got that dread of work feeling, so many felt. Half French, her parents met in France during the last war. Her mother, Celeste, was a nurse and cared for her dad, Alan, while injured in hospital. As he grew stronger, so did their feelings, and Celeste discovered she was pregnant with Kitty. At the end of the war, they left France and married in England, where Celeste adapted easily to her new role as an Anglo-French housewife, with the 'joire de vivre' she gave to everything. She embraced British life, and learning about traditions and culture, even if some of it puzzled her. Yorkshire puddings and gravy were taken to with ease, whilst whelks and cockles, she refused to adopt in the Taylor household.

Katarina, or Kitty as she was known, seemed to be the only one of the three sisters interested in their French heritage. Sophie and Anna were vacuous in Kitty's opinion and fixated on becoming wives and mothers. Sophie was already engaged to a local lad, who was serving on a ship faraway. Anna busied herself chasing

KITTY TAYLOR by Sarah Colliver

anyone who so much as looked her way. Kitty was more interested in building her own future, she didn't need a man for that. Someone who would make demands on her and push her further from her own dreams. The occasional dalliance was fine, but she never let it progress, and a string of disappointed admirers were left in her wake. Her mother always said it was because 'she hadn't met the right one yet, she would be knocked for six when it happened,' but Mother didn't understand. No one did.

Manon named her petite bistro after an old Parisian café, and it was her little slice of France. Kitty felt as though she left Britain once stepping inside, and it was as authentic as you could make it. Even the framed pictures had been brought over before the war. Forced to radically adapt their menu, to account for rationing and shortages, they desperately tried to keep it as French as possible. Luckily for them, they were already known locally for their French onion soup, which had remained as delicious as pre-war, and made up for the lack of pastries, which were few and far between. They always spoke in French together and were delighted when visitors engaged in this way too.

KITTY TAYLOR by Sarah Colliver

"Bonjour, ça va?" Kitty locked the door behind her; there was still an hour before opening time.

"Good morning, all ready to get stuck in?" Manon handed her an apron and offered a red lipstick smile. She always looked the part, and for an older woman, still possessed allure. Kitty often watched as even the younger men became captivated with her French purr and chic appearance. She aspired to be more like her, interesting and beguiling.

"How is your grand-mère? Any better?" Manon understood how much she meant to Kitty.

Kitty sighed and tied her apron with a neat bow. "I wish I could say she was, but I don't think she's ever going to get better. She's unable to say a single word now. It's like she's lost herself and can't find her way back."

Manon gently squeezed her arm and kissed her cheek. "I'm sorry Cherie."

"It's just, well, she was so strong, had so many stories to tell. And she was the only one who would speak in French with me. You know Mother insists that as we live here, we must speak English. Thank God I have you! Why can't she be more like Grand-mère?"

KITTY TAYLOR by Sarah Colliver

"We can only be who we are, your mother isn't all bad, she loves you. Not everyone gets on with their parents, and you have been blessed to be so close to your grand-mère. I do wonder if your mother feels it at times, watching you two together?"

"She doesn't care about that. She has the other two girls to dote on and fuss over. I was the 'mistake'…"

"Cherie! She has never said that to you, why be so hard on her?"

"That's how I feel. We're so different; she and I rub each other the wrong way."

"Well, there's much to get on with here; the best place to be right now and it will distract your thoughts, for a while at least. Now, you make a start on getting these in the oven, it should be to temperature now, and I'll get these tablecloths out on the tables. And don't forget this, we need to keep our standards up!" Manon handed her a red lipstick. She always insisted they both look the part and allow their 'guests' (as opposed to customers) to forget the current world chaos, for their time within her establishment, to be transported to pre-war France, whether they lingered or fleetingly visited.

"Oui, très bien," Kitty answered, curling her mouth around the curves of the words. France coursed through her veins. Despite the occupation, she would rather be there standing her ground with the enemy, than at home, being encouraged to be more 'British' by her mother, who relished in reminding Kitty how utterly ridiculous it was to feel that way. After all, who would choose to live under the occupation, rather than relative safety in Britain? Her mother's words confirmed how misunderstood and alone Kitty felt; increasingly so, since Grand-mère became so ill. Who knew if Britain would be next to fall to the Germans. It was stupid to think that anywhere was safe for anyone now. War was happening to everyone, not just the men who served in uniform, but women and children were also killed daily, by falling bombs.

It was a typical Wednesday afternoon, except for one thing, which could have altered the course of Kitty's life, had Manon reacted in a different way. Heavy rain pounded the bay window, which proudly displayed 'pretend' pre-war delicacies to entice the curiosity of passersby. It was a hard rule of Manon's that once the sign on the door was turned, no more guests were permitted, but on this day as she slid the bolt across the door, a desperate looking couple, running to escape the rain, beseeched her to allow them entry. Perhaps it was the pity she felt as the rain pounded them, or the fact that she was not rushing off on that day as she had food to prepare, or maybe even that there were a couple of her bourguignon portions left, which would be no good the following day, but Kitty never asked why. It was simply, 'one of those things.'

"Bonjour Madame, Monsieur, please come inside and dry off." Manon ushered them inside and took their coats, hanging them on the coat stand to drip by the fire.

Kitty retied her apron, which she was about to remove and pulled out the chair for the immaculate and official looking woman. "Asseyez-vous, please sit down, today's offerings are on the board." She pointed to a blackboard, which was artistically written in both French and English and one of the daily tasks Kitty enjoyed.

KITTY TAYLOR by Sarah Colliver

"Merci Mademoiselle, your French is très bien." The lady's eyes bored into her, which caused Kitty, not one for shying away, to stand taller. She refused to be intimidated.

"Thank you, I will take that as a huge compliment. Can I get you any drinks to begin with?"

"We'll both have coffee, and what do you have left from the board, I can see you were about to close." The gentleman's diction was precise and professional. He was *someone*.

Kitty wanted to answer, that they were already closed, and only re-opened to allow them in, but she knew better and instead spoke politely, "Today, we have two portions of the beef bourguignon left, which is served with frites. Will that be ok for you both?"

"Oui, bon. Merci. What a treat, I had forgotten how much I love frites!" the lady answered, smiled, and then stared intently. Kitty felt as though she were trying to read her mind.

"Merci," Kitty spoke, already on her way to the kitchen. Manon was already preparing the coffee, and

KITTY TAYLOR by Sarah Colliver

Kitty caught her eye. "She's watching my every move," she whispered. "It's making me uneasy."

Manon shook her head, "Not now, later! They might hear you."

Kitty knew not to pursue her concerns. Manon, as a French woman in a foreign country, had fought hard for her impeccable reputation. Kitty understood the part she must play as congenial host, despite her own misgivings.

"Here we are, two coffees." Kitty placed the coffees on the table first and followed with their plates. "All cooked using recipes dating back many years, from the area of Saint-Otto, with a little change, due to the current rationing situation." Kitty shrugged her shoulders in a 'what can you do?' way. "I hope you enjoy."

"Thank you, it smells divine. I haven't eaten since lunch yesterday! It really was such luck we happened to take a wrong turn and found you. Our usual place was bombed out, so you really have lifted our spirits." The lady gave a wide, generous smile, and turned purposefully towards her companion.

KITTY TAYLOR by Sarah Colliver

Kitty was no longer welcome at their table. "Bon appétit," she said, as she wandered back to the kitchen.

And that was it. The moment her life changed, even though Kitty remained blissfully unaware at the time, as her day continued with clearing away after they left, sweeping the floor and wiping the tables. Even as she rode home, with a stale half loaf of bread from Manon in her bicycle basket, hoping it would still be salvageable on arrival home and not sodden, everything felt the same. Funny how the wheels in motion were already clunking away in the background, forging her path, towards the place she loved best.

Wednesdays were always fun because that was dance night at the hall around the corner. Sophie had begun to join them again, since she accepted that it could be years of waiting around for Sidney, and although she loathed to admit it, she craved fun. Playing the yearning fiancé was wearing thin, and she longed to dance. The three girls together turned heads, a similar height, confidence, and long legs, ensured attention. Kitty had to be in the mood for that, whereas Anna absorbed every glance, as a hopeless romantic longing for true love.

"Come on Kitty, all the decent fellas will be taken at this rate." Anna yanked her arm.

"Nothing is less attractive than the whiff of desperation, you remember that. I'm not rushing, go ahead if you're that bothered." She inhaled her cigarette and maintained her pace. "Is that my brooch Sophie?" A small rose encrusted with paste gems sparkled on her left collar.

"You don't really mind, do you?"

"Can't I have anything anymore? You could have asked first, I was going to wear that tonight actually but couldn't find it. Now I know why." Kitty's voice confirmed her irritation.

"It's only a borrow, I promise I won't lose it."

Kitty stared at her sister, she looked different. "Come to think of it, why are you so glammed up tonight? Who are you out to impress and what about Sid?"

Sophie blushed. "I'm not glammed up at all. I fancied a change, nothing more to it."

KITTY TAYLOR by Sarah Colliver

Kitty dropped her cigarette end to the floor, she wasn't about to argue over a brooch, even though it meant more to her than Sophie understood, having been gifted by Grand-mère on a visit to France when she was only ten. "Well, don't lose it."

Sophie kissed her on the cheek and threaded her arm through hers. "Thanks Sis."

The band was in full swing as they arrived at the steps of the Victoria Hall. "My treat tonight girls, courtesy of a nice tip today at work." Kitty smiled at their squeals of delight, as she dropped the money in the tin, and they pushed through the throng of bodies. "Busy tonight, isn't it?"

The bar was three deep, but a familiar face at the end, caught Kitty's eye and she headed towards her, knowing they could queue jump without causing a scene. Once they each had a drink in both hands, to save queuing – they found a table only half-occupied and claimed it as their base.

Kitty took charge. "Right, this is where we come back to. Our drinks are here, and no one leaves without meeting back here first. I'm not spending three hours

KITTY TAYLOR by Sarah Colliver

looking for anyone, this time." They held up their glasses. "Cheers to a night of dancing." Giggles and excitement filled the air, which was a welcome change from the heavy gloom of war.

Anna was first to be swept away, followed by Sophie, whose initial coyness did not fool Kitty for a second. She rolled her eyes at her younger sister.

The deep double bass boomed through her body to her toes, which rhythmically tapped to the beat. She felt free stood alone, watching, with her gift for noticing. Kitty seemed to pick up on little things other people missed. Like the lady dancing with an over-amorous soldier, as her fake smile masked unease at his wandering hands. Or two men leaning in close to talk above the loud music, lingering a little longer than necessary with desire burning in their eyes. A suited man in the shadows of the corner, watching his 'girls' entice unsuspecting drunken Romeos. Kitty felt it was a curse as much as a gift, and sometimes overwhelming. She drained her first drink and swapped her empty glass for the full one.

KITTY TAYLOR by Sarah Colliver

"May I?" A familiar voice from behind whispered in her ear, and a hand took hers, spinning her around to face him.

"Sebastian! You're back!" She kissed him on each cheek and immediately wiped away her lipstick from them.

"Sure am! Now how about that dance you promised me, all those months ago?"

Kitty blushed, she forgot how velvety his brown eyes were, and how tall he stood. He was the only man she could ever fall for, if she were looking for that. "It's so good to see you."

Grabbing her waist, he drew her to the edge of the dance floor and held her gaze. "You look beautiful, as always. How've you been?"

"Same, nothing to report. How about you? You look as though you've been in the sun..."

"Maybe. I couldn't confirm either way." He brushed his lips across hers. "You smell good. I've thought about you a lot..."

KITTY TAYLOR by Sarah Colliver

Kitty slowly kissed him, and her body flooded with desire, which threatened her ability to think. They moved in time to the music, locked in a moment. She wished they were alone again, with his uniform heaped on the floor next to her dress. No one else ever made her feel this way and she knew how her night would end, in bed with Sebastian, chasing away the darkness of the war, and fears of what may yet come.

ALL CHANGE

"I see Sebastian's been back." Manon meticulously polished the glasses as she spoke.

Kitty hung her jacket on the wall, and placed the heavy bag of groceries on the countertop. "You've seen him? Where?" They hadn't met up since she left his room to sneak home during a raid. Her parents drove her mad, but they didn't deserve the worry of where she was. Most people were scared to be out amongst the chaos and destruction during air raids, but she never felt more alive than when her senses flooded with adrenaline. She managed to run the entire journey home, where she found her family squeezed in to the Anderson shelter with paled relieved faces to see her appear. She ignored their berating and probing questions, answering time after time, "everything is ok, I'm here now."

"He popped in for a coffee, although I suspect he was looking for you, yesterday after you left."

Kitty felt a mixture of disappointment and relief. Their time together was always enjoyable, and he made her feel desirable and capable. But to become entangled at this stage, would ruin everything. Her feelings were conflicting. She had plans, and a man would prevent them from being realised. Her dream was to create a shop back in Saint-Otto, the village where her ancestors were from. She would call it 'Delphine's,' after her grand-mère. She even knew the exact shade of blue she would paint the woodwork and shutters and was determined to save every penny towards it.

"Do you think he will be back in?" Kitty adjusted her hair in the ornate mirror beside the counter and touched up her lipstick.

KITTY TAYLOR by Sarah Colliver

"Sorry Cherie, no. He was reporting back for duty today. Did you get everything we needed, or do we need to change our menu?"

"Today it's all there, I had to promise Mr Bavistock a free coffee when he next comes in to secure the extra onions."

"Good thinking! You look disappointed. Is it Sebastian? Did you manage to see him at all this time?"

Kitty blushed, as her mind briefly led her back to the thought of his naked body. "We caught up a week ago. I'm fine, just wondering when he will be back, that's all." But she had to acknowledge inwardly, disappointment lay in the pit of her hungry stomach. It was unsettling, as she fought so hard not to become entangled, but he always knew what to say and do, until she was powerless to resist.

A knock on the door, which lay between a polite bang and a forceful pound, stopped their conversation and turned their heads towards the sound. Neither said a word, but both wondered who it could be.

"I'll go; you carry on," Kitty spoke as she headed through the tables, still piled with chairs from the recent floor mopping. As she approached the door, unease crept across her. It was the couple from the previous week and pre-empting their question, she called to Manon, "Are we allowing them in again? It's still early?"

"Can we come in? We only have this opportunity for a break," the lady spoke through the glass of the door, in perfect French.

"Let them in," Manon sighed. "But warn them what we can offer is limited at this precise moment." Manon wiped flour from her face and smiled wearily.

Kitty opened the door and locked it behind the guests. "Welcome back Madame, Monsieur. Please come in. Our menu is limited at this moment, as we are still working on today's food." Kitty pulled down two chairs from the table. "One moment, I will wipe it and get a fresh cloth, also, please be careful as the floor was recently mopped, and we would not want you to slip."

"Thank you, you are most generous. Two coffees and do you have any of that bourguignon, that authentic one which we had last time? It was so delicious."

KITTY TAYLOR by Sarah Colliver

Kitty straightened the crisp white cloth. "I'm sorry, no. It won't be ready for a few hours, but I can offer you French onion soup, it is yesterday's, but we have a good reputation for this dish around here, and personally, I think it is better the next day."

"Can we have the pommes frites again?" The lady brought her hands together as if in prayer.

"I will ask for you, one moment please."

Kitty hurried out to the kitchen area. "I don't know what it is, but she unsettles me. I feel like she has things to say but is holding back."

"They look tired I think, Cherie. It is more like they are busy, worn out. This is a sanctuary and like we always say, we want our guests to feel cared for and safe while they visit us. Non?"

Kitty smiled and nodded. "They want the soup but with some frites, what shall I say?"

"How about you put their tray of coffee together, and I make a fresh batch of frites, and then you and I can sit and enjoy some too, oui?"

KITTY TAYLOR by Sarah Colliver

Kitty nodded and acknowledged her rumbling tummy at the thought. "It's a strange time to be eating soup and frites."

"Perhaps they've been working all night, the world is upside down right now, nothing is as it should be."

"True," Kitty smiled. Manon was always so calm and knew what to say. The difference in their age, she supposed.

"Pour vous, here is your coffee, Manon is cooking your frites, and here is your soup. Can I help in any other way Madame?"

The man nodded ever so slightly, some sort of affirmation to the lady. So insignificant, that it would be missed by any onlooker without Kitty's ability to notice.

"Non, merci," she responded.

Kitty straightened her apron, as Manon delivered the frites, to groans of pleasure from the guests. The food smelled delicious and could provoke stomach grumbles from even the fullest tummies. "If you need anything else, please let us know."

KITTY TAYLOR by Sarah Colliver

Kitty busied herself in preparation for opening. Having cleaned the blackboard, she skilfully wrote the day's offerings in French, whilst monitoring the guests who were then readying to leave.

"Mademoiselle, that was even more delicious than before. Do you make this food?" the lady called across, again speaking in French.

"Oui, my grand-mère taught me, it goes back generations, but I am afraid they are secret family recipes which I cannot share!" Kitty hung the finished board back up on the wall, ready for opening and headed towards the table. "You are finished?"

"Thank you, yes." The lady put her knife and fork together and lay her used napkin on the table. "Have you ever been to France?"

"Yes, many times. I used to visit my grand-mère before she moved here to live with us. I learned everything from her. We only ever speak French together. One day I will go back, for good probably." Kitty balanced the dirty plates and cutlery with expertise.

Leaning in close to Kitty, she whispered, "Please, come and see me at this address, tomorrow at 4pm. I might have an idea which will interest you and your recipes." She pushed a business card into Kitty's apron pocket.

Kitty blushed, perhaps she was a publisher, or running articles in newspapers. She may be able to earn extra money, towards her dream. Kitty nodded, despite the unease creeping across her. Manon was occupied at the oven, and seemed not to have noticed a thing. It felt secretive, and instinct told her not to acknowledge this exchange to Manon. Once again, the mysterious couple tipped well, and she knew that Manon, in her generosity, would be happy for Kitty to keep it all.

Her own feature, her own recipes. But could she share them, should she share them? And would she be betraying Grand-mère if she did? She didn't have much time to consider everything before the meeting and pondered the offer as she cleared their table away.

Manon placed a large bowl of frites on the counter. "Here, let's eat these before we open up. We can't serve others with a smile if our own tummies are grumbling!"

KITTY TAYLOR by Sarah Colliver

Grand-mère lay as comfortably as they could make it, in the back room, which they had changed from the dining room into a cosy bedroom for her. The quilt, made by generations of her family, was gifted on her wedding day, and kept the chills away from her paper-thin shell. The only spanner in the works was that they could not move her during the raids. Kitty refused to leave her initially, but after her father reasoning that it would be more detrimental to move Grand-mère than for her to take her chances in the house, she reluctantly agreed.

Kitty kissed and squeezed her father tight on the day he revealed the invention he had built – a little like an aviary for birds, which they could fit over Grand-mère's bed during raids. Although Kitty wasn't stupid and knew it wasn't guaranteed to protect her from every eventuality, it meant they hadn't abandoned her to save their own skin but considered her safety and worth too. It may prevent wounds from shrapnel or flying glass at least. In Kitty's mind it was worth taking up half of the room when not in use, although Celeste moaned about having to clean around it.

On entering, Kitty thought a vague smile crept across Grand-mère's wrinkly face.

KITTY TAYLOR by Sarah Colliver

"C'est moi, Grand-mère, it's Katarina." Kitty clasped her stiff hand in her own and gently kissed it. Grand-mère was the only one who called her by her real name. "I miss you so much." She spoke in whispered French, hoping for a moment of privacy with her beloved grand-mère.

"I think I may have a way to earn more money, for my shop...but...it possibly means sharing our recipes. Could I really do that? Would you give your blessing?"

Kitty stared at her face, which was carved with wrinkles and peppered with paled mismatched liver spots. The woman who taught her to cook, who patiently listened to her woes and took every opportunity to be in her company, was now locked somewhere deep within her tired, old shell. Still, Kitty searched for an acknowledgement, anything that might offer reassurance. But her blank face stared up at the ceiling.

"Please, I need your help, I can't do this without you." She was at her weakest when it involved Grand-mère, it was as though the love and devotion she felt, melted Kitty's tough core, and there was nothing she could do about it. "I must go and meet her tomorrow. I don't know whether to agree or not, I need you to give me a sign...please?"

She kissed Grand-mère's hand again and rubbed it across her cheek, wet with fresh tears as she wished for one more conversation, one more baking lesson, one more steaming coffee together...

    Kitty's glum mood seemed to seep out and contaminate everything in her path. It was one of those days which never really got light and weighed oppressively on those already struggling to 'keep calm and carry on'. She sighed as she passed the first of many bombsites and wondered how many would die before the end of the war came. Would she be one of them- buried beneath a pile of rubble? She shrugged away the intrusive thoughts, berating her for doing nothing to contribute to victory. Her mother would often remind her that lifting the morale with delicious cuisine *was* a way of fighting. But Kitty always sighed beneath her breath at how patronising her mother sounded, after all she wasn't fifteen anymore. She knew that Mother only said this, because she and Dad liked Kitty working safely in a café, as opposed to in uniform.

Tucked inside her leather satchel were the recipes, although despite being enroute to the meeting, she had not decided whether she would be willing to share her precious secrets. It was out of curiosity more than anything that enticed her to Baker Street, and she wondered if the name alone was a sign that this was her destiny after all.

Kitty arrived at number 64, where a suited gentleman stood, as though awaiting her arrival. "Name?"

"Katarina Taylor."

"Through here and up to the first floor, second door on the right." He pushed the heavy front door and held it open.

Kitty felt a swell of excitement in her stomach, the feeling as though you are on the cusp of something, and she stifled a wide smile by chewing her lip. The staircase was smart, with a dark wood trim. She slowed down her walk, to appear in control, fighting the urge to fly up the stairs two at a time. Although the hallways were devoid of people, chatter and the clatter of typewriters echoed from behind the many closed doors. She straightened her skirt and shook her hair, before knocking on the door, as instructed.

"Come in."

Kitty pushed open the door of a small office overlooking the busy street below. It was the lady from the café. "Hello again." Kitty reached out her hand.

"Sylvia Mills, hello again Kitty Taylor."

Kitty swallowed her words, which were obsolete it seemed, as Sylvia already knew who she was.

"Don't look so puzzled. I don't invite anyone here without some preliminary background checks, please sit down. Drink?"

Kitty shook her head and perched on the seat opposite Sylvia. Her mind whirled as she digested what she had revealed. Why would she do that for some old recipes?

"Smoke?" Kitty took a cigarette, and Sylvia lit it for her. "You really have no inkling as to why I have invited you? What's in the case?"

KITTY TAYLOR by Sarah Colliver

Kitty blushed, what was going on? She felt stupid but with no idea why. "Recipes. You said you wanted to speak to me about them. I thought maybe you were a publisher, wanted to do a piece on traditional French food?"

Sylvia coughed, but Kitty was sure it was to stifle a giggle. Kitty shifted in the chair suddenly aware that she was in a building, with no idea who this woman was. The only person she had confided in was Grand-mère, who could no longer communicate, and if anything were to happen to her, no one would ever find her. And then, her senses kicked in and she scanned the room. Nothing personal, it was generic and could belong to anyone. The desk was empty except for a half full crystal ash tray, an open packet of cigarettes with a fancy lighter engraved with a swirly SM, and a brown personnel file, which had the name 'Katarina Taylor' written on the front.

"Why do you have a file on me?" She stood up, anger flared her nostrils. "Who are you? I've done nothing wrong, who gave you permission to create a whole file on me?"

Sylvia remained in her seat silently and stared at Kitty.

KITTY TAYLOR by Sarah Colliver

"Do you know how rude you appear to be? You invited me here, implying that you are interested in my cooking, and then laugh at me. Yes, I did notice that stifled giggle- you didn't hide it well at all. Now, you sit staring at me, as though I am the one behaving inappropriately." Kitty stubbed out the cigarette in the ashtray and turned to leave, hurrying towards the door.

"Wait," Sylvia ordered.

Kitty stopped.

"Come back and sit down. We have a lot to get through today and you are going to want to listen, that much I know."

"This is strange, this whole set up..." Kitty shook her head.

"I know it must seem that way right now, but you will understand by the time you leave here today, what this is about. I promise." Sylvia smiled and pointed towards the seat, "Please sit down again."

KITTY TAYLOR by Sarah Colliver

Kitty returned to her chair, placed her case on the floor and crossed her legs. Her demeanour screamed, 'I'm waiting,' yet she remained silent.

"Tell me about your plans for the future, France, the shop..."

"How do you know about them?"

"I can only reveal what you need to know from this point onwards. Now, tell me," Sylvia replied.

"I'm going to live in Saint-Otto, where my family are from, and using Grand-mère's recipes, will create a traditional shop, to sell our delicacies."

"You have visited Saint-Otto four times?"

Kitty nodded, "Oui."

"You speak excellent French. You're angry about the occupation and wish you could be more use to the war effort."

"I notice you are no longer asking me questions, more stating facts about me." Kitty raised her eyebrows.

KITTY TAYLOR by Sarah Colliver

"Kitty I have your entire life in this file. I know, for instance, that you enjoy the company of men without craving attachments. And I know you dislike lavender scent and plum jam. These are only two examples."

Kitty blushed. She really did know everything. "Okay, I believe you and you clearly approve of me, otherwise I doubt very much I would be sat here right now. So, let's discuss the reason I'm here, because the rest is irrelevant if I don't agree to whatever you are going to ask of me."

"You have spirit too. I like that." Sylvia paused but her eyes remained fixed on Kitty. "Okay. We want to send you over to France."

Kitty laughed, "France is occupied."

Sylvia nodded and held Kitty's gaze. "We need authentic French-speaking women, to live in France, and become our eyes and ears behind enemy lines."

"Jesus. You really mean it, don't you."

Sylvia nodded. "You can write and speak French, you are pretty, and it hasn't escaped my notice that you have an eye for detail. You are a wasted asset, cooking in a small back street café in London, no matter how good the food is."

A heavy silence sat between them. Kitty was usure if she had been insulted or complimented.

"Interested?" Sylvia smiled. "Actually, don't say anything for a moment, let it sink in. I'll get some coffee brought in to us."

Kitty's gut feeling was right after all, something big was looming, but not for one second had she imagined it to be this big. Every ounce of her being wanted to agree immediately. Two years ago she would have answered already. But with a little more maturity comes wisdom, and she needed a moment, because this was life-altering.

"Come in," Sylvia answered the knock at the door and an older looking lady with small glasses and grey hair, placed a tray onto the side of the desk. "Thank you." Sylvia smiled at the lady who nodded and exited swiftly.

Sylvia handed Kitty a cup. "What do you say, first thoughts?"

KITTY TAYLOR by Sarah Colliver

Kitty sipped the steaming liquid, it wasn't as nice at the way they make theirs in the café, but she was glad of the prop to bide her more time. "It's quite a surprise, not one I expected."

"I understand, but I need to know your gut reaction."

"Okay, my immediate reaction, is of course, yes. But you already know this, because you know everything about me. So, it's not a gamble really, you must have been sure I would react this way, to invite me here in the first place."

"You have a good instinct. How will you explain your uniform, I cannot imagine your parents accepting this huge change, knowing how much you love your job alongside Manon?"

Kitty again marvelled at how much Sylvia knew about her. She swallowed a mouthful of coffee. "Uniform?"

"Yes, you will be working under the cover of the WAAF, would that be a problem?"

Kitty's lip quivered; her parents would not be supportive of that. She sighed.

"It is an issue then?"

KITTY TAYLOR by Sarah Colliver

"They always said they wanted us girls to stay away from the uniform roles, this could cause me a big problem with my family. Although, at 23 there isn't a lot they can do about it."

"You don't want to be on bad terms with them, Kitty, these things have a way of playing on your mind while in the field. Let me think, okay, how about we say that you will be training at a catering college initially, for gifted chefs. Then, once your training is completed, you can say that everyone on the course were recruited, and you wanted to do your bit. Less of a jump from your café job to uniform, and perhaps easier to digest if you have been a way for a while. How does that sound?"

"We will soon find out." Kitty smiled, but she could already imagine her mother crying hysterically and ringing her hands together.

"I'm not going to lie. If you agree to this, there is no promise you will come home, I mean we cannot guarantee your safety, Kitty. It will involve training in both combat and intelligence. You cannot tell a soul about this. You will be alone, both here and once in France, with this secret. Can you manage that?"

KITTY TAYLOR by Sarah Colliver

There was no going back, not now her mind was open to this possibility of returning to her beloved France, to fight the enemy. How could she ever return to being 'just a waitress' as her sisters called her so often. This meeting had already changed her, and a whole new realm of choices, possibilities and danger lay ahead. "Where do I sign?"

CAMOFLAGE & RED LIPSTICK

The khaki uniforms were itchy, but after a few days training, she realised their worth. The material was hardwearing and practical. Her legs ached from the vigorous exercising and lack of sleep. Wasn't sleep supposed to help your body recover? Since arriving a week previously, she had barely got three hours a night.

Her code name was Giselle Lavigne, and she was unable to utter a single word about Kitty, it was as though she left her at home. She imagined Kitty sat with Grand-mère, holding her hand, as she got steadily worse. She was unlikely to live out the month, the doctor said. It

KITTY TAYLOR by Sarah Colliver

broke Kitty's heart when she received her orders, and her parents were angry and bewildered. 'Where had this sudden change come from? Who had influenced her? Where was she going?' Their questions were endless. Her cover story was that she had been discovered by a leading chef, who offered a place at her cookery training college for gifted people – and if the exams were passed, she could be a top patisserie chef in one of the big establishments, like the Ritz. Manon cried when she told her the news and begged her not to go. Her eyes flashed doubt in her story, and Kitty was convinced she suspected something. But she never said a word and once she dried her tears, in typical Manon fashion, she reapplied her lipstick and straightened her hair. "You must do what you think is right Cherie, I will not stand in your way. But I will miss you so much...as will our regulars who visit only for your dishes!" Kitty loved that Manon affectionately called her Cherie, and she felt more like an aunt or older sister than employer. They would always be friends.

"Lavigne, stop daydreaming and get up that rope!"

"Sir!" Kitty had never felt so exhausted and yet, despite the rope burns, she managed to pull herself up and down the rope until the Sargent was satisfied with her effort. She hoped her hands wouldn't be permanently scarred, but it was likely.

"Now, before you call it a day, I want a lap of the property, two miles in total, no short cuts, I have spies watching you. Remember, running might save your life one day, so this is as important as learning to fire a gun. I want your best times too, imagine Jerry is chasing you. Last recruit back cleans the toilet. Three, two, GO!"

Kitty sprinted off, she had always been a good runner, and although she had to dig deeper due to how tired she was, she knew she wouldn't be last.

"Hey Giselle, fancy a drink before dinner?" Dominique asked in between gasps.

Kitty had promised herself to always remember this was not her real life, and she had to think like Giselle. She could reveal nothing about Kitty, which made conversing hard, and she mostly kept to herself so far. "Maybe, depends how tired I am later, as I want a bath too and really need to get my head down."

"Mind if I run with you, could do with trying to keep my pace up, I'd rather not clean the loos."

KITTY TAYLOR by Sarah Colliver

Kitty looked at her new companion, Dominique. She had a small scar above her eyebrow and long eyelashes. Her hair was dyed blonde and her voice clipped and posh.

"No-one wants to clean the loos, that's the point!" Kitty laughed and picked up her pace, to see if Dominique could keep up. Something about her felt off, but then it was like everything was upside down, like Alice falling into Wonderland. Because no one was who they really are, but everyone was on guard, hiding themselves, practicing for the main event when their lives would depend on it. So, it was difficult to know whether to trust the usual instincts or not. After all, she herself was not acting normal either.

Soon Dominque floundered and Kitty was again running alone, ahead of everyone. The perimeter gave her the opportunity to admire the rolling Scottish hills, swathed with heather and trickling brooks. One day she would visit, when it wasn't wartime, and enjoy lying beside one of the streams listening to the water and birdsong. They were far from the nearest village. Inverness was twelve miles away; distance was essential for maintaining the secrecy of what this exquisite manor house was really teaching.

KITTY TAYLOR by Sarah Colliver

"Good work Lavigne. First in – get yourself washed up and then onto the hall for lectures for 1600 hours."

"Sir." If she were lucky, she could make it in time for a quick cup of tea before class began.

Manon had sent Kitty off with one of her best French silk blouses, and a pre-war red lipstick from Paris, to keep up appearances. Kitty swooned over the blouse, having always wanted one, but determined to save every penny for her future, made do with swaps and cheaper items. Not that one like that could be obtained now, as it was from Paris. She was surprised when she tried it on, as her first thought was that Sebastian would like her in it, but she squashed the thought, angry with herself. She may never even see him again, this time not because he may not return, but because she knew danger lay ahead of her too now. She had more to worry about, than thoughts of an unobtainable man, who would realistically not fit into the future picture she had already painted for herself.

She buttoned up the blouse, which proved tricky because of her sore hands, and applied lipstick, smiling

KITTY TAYLOR by Sarah Colliver

as Manon's voice popped into her head, 'We must keep up appearances Cherie.' Pinning her hair up, she hoped that it would be less obvious how badly it needed washing. She looked tired, but despite her aching muscles, a fire burned in her, which could not be extinguished by any amount of physical training. All that lay between her and getting over to France was this course and her resolve.

"Hello?" A knock on the door followed, it was Dominique.

"Coming now," Kitty answered and hurried out onto the landing. "I'm starving!"

"Me too, but I've been longing for a brandy all day, smoke?"

Kitty took a cigarette and they paused at the top of the ornate sweeping staircase to light them. Everyone smoked, it got them through the darker moments. The descriptions of how brutal the torture could be if the Gestapo caught them, was not for the faint hearted. A few recruits left shortly after those lectures. Luckily, Kitty seemed to possess the ability to compartmentalise and lock it away. That didn't mean she wasn't acutely aware of the danger, more that she could focus on the job, as opposed to the threat.

"I really quite fancy him." Dominique nodded towards a tall, slight chap with delicate features. "What about you, anyone in your life?

"Each to their own, but he doesn't do it for me, I like a bit more meat on the bones." Kitty avoided her question, determined to complete the challenge to give nothing away.

"At least we won't be competing for him, I suppose. That's a French design." She pointed to Kitty's blouse.

"Is it? I hadn't noticed. Now how about that drink, it's almost dinner time?"

None of the male recruits turned her head, none were even worth enjoying a night with. Romantic encounters were not encouraged, but they were consenting adults, and no guards were posted outside of their rooms. She was too exhausted anyway, and Sebastian was a tough act to follow in that department. They shared a chemistry, which ignited at first glance, and not once, had they spent time together without ending up in bed.

KITTY TAYLOR by Sarah Colliver

It was undeniable and thoroughly enjoyable. Kitty blushed recalling their most recent encounter.

"I'm going to seduce him, tonight," Dominique whispered behind her hand and smiled.

Kitty laughed, "That sounds so formal." But she was really laughing because she had clocked him eyeing up another recruit, a male one. "Good luck with that."

Opting for the local whiskey, Kitty inhaled the oaky scent before sipping it. The golden liquid burned her throat, and she coughed. It would likely function as anaesthesia on her fatigued body, but the promise of a hearty meal wafted past her nose. Dinner was announced and her stomach grumbled in response.

Everyone dashed to the dining room, despite their manners and reserve. It felt as though they were not eating enough calories to satisfy their hunger and compensate for their training. It was all very clever, Kitty thought. Training aside, there were tests and lessons every minute. They were being surveyed she surmised. How would they cope on little sleep, not quite enough food, and she even suspected every little mishap, like the water not working or their dinners being delayed, to see what would make them snap. She wondered if Dominique was a plant, to test how much information people would offer about themselves. It was hard to tell in the topsy-turvy world. But that was the point; they were slipping into France, to act a part, in an unfamiliar world of occupation, where you could trust no one.

Dinner was over quickly; their hunger quickened the process, and despite best efforts to make small talk, one by one they retired to bed for some much-needed sleep. Kitty sighed, drifting off into her safe place: her shop in Saint-Otto on the square with the bistro tables and chairs, beneath the shade of the trees....

Suddenly her door burst open, and she was hauled from her bed. For a second, she was unsure if she were awake or dreaming, but the force of her hair being yanked, confirmed the pain was real, as her cold bare feet dragged behind her. She blinked away her sleep and fought to gain clarity on what this was, as they threw her to the floor of a dank, sewage stinking chamber. Her eyes fought to adjust to the darkness, and the door slammed shut. She held her breath to see if she could hear if anyone else was with her. From behind someone stood still, only their rhythmic breaths

KITTY TAYLOR by Sarah Colliver

gave them away. She spun around to face the sound and shouted, "Who are you and what do you want with me?"

"Shut your dirty, traitor mouth," a voice screamed. "Do not speak unless I ask you to."

This was the interrogation. They all heard rumours that this might happen. She must hold her nerve. He grabbed her chin in a vice like hold and brought his face so close to hers she could feel his breath. "Who are you?" he whispered.

"Giselle Lavigne."

"Liar," he shrieked. "We know who you are, and who your family are too. I can kill them all with one word of command." He shoved her body away with such force, that she fell backwards.

A bright light switched on and blinded her, as he again approached and whispered, "You can save them. All of them, especially the grand-mère you love so much. And those pretty sisters of yours, what I could do to them...just tell me what you know."

KITTY TAYLOR by Sarah Colliver

Kitty's stomach heaved at the mention of her family. She had put them at risk. It hadn't occurred to her that doing this would endanger them. Panic threatened to blind her, but she squeezed her fists and dug her nail into the palm of her sore hand, to bring her back to the moment. "My name is Giselle Lavigne..."

"You are a liar!" He slapped her face, and she reeled from the force. She regained her balance and stared into his cold blue eyes.

"My name is Giselle Lavigne."

He grabbed her hair and yanked her face away from him towards the side of the room, where a dentist chair stood. It looked eerily out of place, complete with every silver instrument you could imagine would be needed for extractions. Her heart thumped and she was sure he could hear the sound, as her dinner gurgled up into her throat. Not that! She couldn't manage that. She closed her eyes and tried to think, to bide some time, but it was clear she didn't call the shots, as she was grabbed under each arm pit and strapped to the chair. She swallowed her screams but could not prevent her silent tears.

"Now, perhaps you might feel more favourable about sharing your information, Kitty."

She bit at the fingers which fought to hold open her mouth and shook her head violently. "Okay. Okay. Please let go of my face, I will tell you everything…"

FLYING COLOURS

Sylvia was less reserved this time. She warmly pulled Kitty into the office which she had commandeered in the grand Scottish house and beamed with pride. "I always knew you were made of strong stuff, but Kitty, you exceeded all of my expectations!"

"So does this mean I passed?" Kitty could hardly breathe.

"With flying colours, top of the group actually. Your 'phys' was above average, but the intelligence part brought you right to the top. You have an eye for detail and that instinct cannot be taught. If only it could be…"

KITTY TAYLOR by Sarah Colliver

"Thank you." Kitty beamed and relief flooded her.

"Your interrogation, have you been ok since? That part is pretty rough."

"I've been wondering if I could have done anything differently. Only thing I have decided to do is to keep my cyanide capsule on me even when I sleep, is that possible? When I saw that dentist chair, I thought it was over for me and as I went through my options, I ruled it out as a choice at the time, because I wouldn't have had a chance to grab it."

"We can arrange to have a pocket made in your brassiere, to fit your capsule in, if you would like?"

Kitty nodded and accepted the cigarette Sylvia offered.

"Any bruises?"

"Nothing a little make-up can't cover up." Kitty exhaled the smoke and smiled.

"You gave nothing away; the information you offered was nonsense and yet you were utterly believable."

"Were you there too? I didn't see you..." Kitty puzzled.

KITTY TAYLOR by Sarah Colliver

"It's a specially adapted room so that you can be monitored and assessed. You displayed such courage Kitty." Sylvia smiled, and her eyes pooled with pride. "You know, I must ask this. Do you want to proceed, to continue forwards? Because things are about to move pretty quickly."

"I wouldn't have gone through the last few weeks if I wasn't sure. I would rather get on with it than build up nerves waiting, but will I get to visit home first?"

"Good, I can't pretend that I wouldn't have been devastated if you had backed out now, although I would have still thought you incredible for what you have achieved. Yes, you can have the weekend at home, but I must emphasise that you cannot speak of anything you have encountered or allude to where you may be heading. You must say that you will be coming back up here to join your fellow WAAFS."

Kitty nodded and the enormity of her new normal began to sink in. Lying about everything would be difficult, but it would have been much harder to keep from Grand-mère had she been well. Tears pricked her eyes at the thought of holding her hand once more.

KITTY TAYLOR by Sarah Colliver

"You have much to digest, I can see that. But let's both take a moment to acknowledge you Kitty. You are an asset to your countries. I believe there is no such thing as coincidence, but things happen for a reason. We were meant to cross paths. You were meant to do this. Now, enjoy your down-time, and be back here for Monday 0800 hours. A train leaves in two hours, so you'll need to hurry along. Oh, before you go, here are your return tickets, and also this might be useful in convincing your family about your story," Sylvia handed her a box. "To show them how busy you have been in the kitchen."

Kitty opened it to find a mixture of cakes, and smiled. "They'd better taste delicious if I'm passing them off as my own, I don't want my reputation sullied."

KITTY TAYLOR by Sarah Colliver

HOME

Kitty wandered along the busy street from the station, bustling from the recent disembarkation of the arriving trains. She felt changed from when she was last home, as though she had lived a whole lifetime whilst away. It was good to stretch her legs after the laborious journey, despite how mucky and dusty the air felt. The area had taken a pounding from raids and everywhere seemed so unfamiliar. The recent bombings had obliterated large swathes of houses on her childhood streets. The useful corner shop, visited daily by local families, still displayed an 'OPEN' sign, despite the blown-out windows and piles of rubble around, where houses once stood.

Kitty panicked for a moment, that perhaps her home was gone too, that her family could be dead. But Sylvia would have warned her, they knew everything it seemed, and that thought helped chase away her fears.

Her blood boiled at the destruction and death, but she calmed herself with soothing reminders that she would soon be fighting the Germans first-hand. But before she could tackle the enemy, she had to weather the impending storm: arriving home in uniform. She straightened up and smoothed her skirt.

"Well I never…here she is, back from her la-de-da college! But why are you in a WAAF uniform?" Kitty swung around to see Gladys, the shopkeeper, waving her broom.

"Yes, that's right, WAAFs. We all seemed to have been recruited, the college was closed at the end of the term."

Gladys looked her up and down. "Glad to be back? What do you make of all this then? Not much left of the street now is there? Lucky for you, your road is still standing. Ooh I could swing for that bloody Hitler." She prodded her broom in the air. "If I could get my hands on him."

Kitty smiled and imagined the scene. Adolf Hitler running away from Gladys and her witchy broom, like the kids do when they've been caught up to mischief. Oh, how she would love to see that.

"It's hard to get your bearings Gladys. It all looks so different. Many lost?"

KITTY TAYLOR by Sarah Colliver

"Not as many as there could've been...but enough." She wiped fresh tears with a hanky from her overall pocket. She had worn the same mint green overalls for Kitty's whole life. Maybe she never took them off? But Gladys, her broom, her green overalls, and warm disposition, were part of the geography of the area. An area which seemed to be disappearing fast. Kitty was glad to be back where her past was anchored, even if it was a flying visit.

"Send my regards to your parents, and Delphine." Gladys waved and wandered back inside, to continue sweeping up.

"Cheerio." Kitty headed away from the rubble, back onto the in-tact pavement, towards her row of terraced houses. They were bigger on Gloster road than the dockers' cottages, and although from the front seemed small, the rooms were generous in size, and the houses reached on back like a warren. The six of them had fitted comfortably at number 7 for many years.

Although Kitty had slept on and off, soothed by the motion of the train and rickety rack of the rails, she needed a solitary moment to push away Giselle, and allow Kitty back. Kitty, who supposedly spent hours

KITTY TAYLOR by Sarah Colliver

cooking in a hot kitchen, under the watchful eyes of her tutor, at her exclusive college in Scotland. She rehearsed the details like lines in a play.

"Hello?" She pushed open the red front door, which looked tired and worn with bomb dust clinging to the paintwork like a parasite, and headed through to the kitchen where everyone usually gathered.

"What a lovely surprise, you didn't say you were coming home!" her mother called from the sitting room and poked her head out onto the hallway. Her mouth fell open. "What are you wearing? I don't understand."

"Don't start! Please let me at least get in the door before you start wailing."

"Don't be so rude Kitty. What do you expect? When did this happen?" She pointed to the pristine uniform. "Why didn't you write and tell me? I'm your mother after all. Don't I at least deserve a letter?"

"Which question would you like me to answer first? Or might I at least be offered a cup of tea before I begin?"

KITTY TAYLOR by Sarah Colliver

Her mother shook her head and stormed into the kitchen. Kitty followed. "They shut the course down because of the war. No one on the course refused. They have changed the college into a training base for WAAFs. So, I'm only here for the weekend and need to get the overnight train back up. We can spend our time fighting or make the most of it. That's up to you."

"But why couldn't you have stayed with Manon, you loved that job, and she would have you back in a heartbeat."

Kitty pondered her job at the café, which seemed like a million years ago. She folded her arms and leaned against the fireplace, staring at her mother who was manhandling the floral china tea set, which was bearing the brunt of her frustration as she prepared a tray of tea.

She turned to Kitty; her weary smile did not hide the sadness in her eyes. "It's... well, I *know* what happens to soldiers. I've seen more uniforms stained with blood, than you can imagine. It still haunts me. Your father, he can never forget what he witnessed in the Somme. Whenever I see uniforms, it takes me straight back there." She wiped her nose with a handkerchief and sucked in a deep breath. "Now, let me make a pot of tea. You look exhausted. You're wasting away. Turn around and let me look at you!" Concern filled her eyes.

That thought had not occurred to Kitty and guilt tinged her irritation. "Tea would be lovely, and look, we were even allowed to bring what we have been working on, home. A real treat! They seem to be able to get extra rations up there for our lessons, but it unfortunately doesn't stretch to the canteen, which I guess is why I have lost weight..." Now she understood the importance of visual evidence to back up her stories. The SOE really did think of everything it seemed. She opened the box to distract her mother from her shrinking waistline. "See."

"You made these? Oh Kitty! Can we wait for the others to come home and then we can celebrate together, Sidney is on leave too." Tears once again pricked her eyes.

Kitty's head spun and was already full to capacity, yet she had been home precisely five minutes. "While you make the tea, I will go in and see Grand-mère."

KITTY TAYLOR by Sarah Colliver

"Okay, I'll bring your tea through love. Oh, and it really is good to see you." She kissed Kitty on both cheeks and smiled. "What do you think your father will make of this?"

"He'll have to deal with it too, this is who I am now." Their eyes locked for a moment, before Kitty shifted uncomfortably and turned towards Grand-mère's room. She peeked through the crack in the door, and watched for a minute as Grand-mère lay still in her bed, beneath her beloved quilt. Kitty sniffed away her tears and pushed the chair up close to the bed. "C'est moi, Katarina." She took her skeletal hand and kissed it over and over, before kissing her cheeks. "I have so much to tell you, where I've been and where I'm going. But not now in case we are heard. I've missed you so much, I kept pretending that part of me was still sitting here like this, holding your hand. That is what got me through."

"Here love, your tea." Her mother handed Kitty a porcelain cup with a slight chip on the handle.

"Thanks."

KITTY TAYLOR by Sarah Colliver

"Good to have you home, it's not the same here without you, Kitty." She offered a small smile, but her eyes remained sad.

"How are you, anyway, with everything that's going on?" Kitty softened her voice. Her mother was looking older and worn out and dabbed at her weeping eyes.

We're losing her you know, your grand-mère."

"We lost her months ago, this is no life…I would hate to get like this, and she would too, I know it. If she could speak now, she would beg us to let her go." The words hung in the air, and Kitty realised how harsh they sounded. She cursed her own insensitivity.

Her mother sobbed. Kitty's guilt at her own lack of emotion towards her meant she had nothing to add to the conversation. She was sad for her, she was losing her own mother after all, but so much resentment sat like a gulf between them. Grand-mère was Kitty's best friend, her confident, teacher, and a steady guiding hand. Kitty's grieving began long ago when Grand-mère began to sit so quietly in her chair, and refused to get out of bed or drink her hot coffee. Kitty knew then that piece by piece, she was being stolen away from her.

KITTY TAYLOR by Sarah Colliver

The tea was too sweet, and on a usual day she would have moaned about it, but she said nothing.

"There's a little sugar in it because you look like you need building up." Her mother managed to say through her sobs.

Kitty nodded and half smiled. "Can I have a little while alone with her? I'm home for such a short time and fear this may be my last few days with her."

She nodded and silently stood up, taking her empty cup, she sniffled out of the room and closed the door.

"Grand-mère," Kitty whispered, "I need to tell you what's happening, I passed my course and now they are sending me to France. Can you believe it? I had to train in setting explosives, firing a gun and, wait for it, this is the best part, I came top of my class, it was my interrogation that did it."

Grand-mère's hand moved. Kitty stood and leaned over to face her, locking into her eyes, searching for something, anything resembling acknowledgement of the words she spoke. "Can you hear me?" Kitty whispered. "Did you move your hand? Is it because you are worried for me? Because I must do this for you and me. There really isn't any backing out now."

A single tear rolled from the corner of Grand-mère's eye down her cheek and onto the pillow.

"Don't be sad! You would do the same I know you would! This is my destiny." Kitty kissed her wrinkled cheeks. "I love you so much, thank you for making me the woman I am today. It's all because of you." Kitty thought that for a moment Grand-mère knew her, recognised her face, before sinking back into her personal oblivion. But that was enough for her, to know she heard what she said. It was like giving her blessing, and that meant luck would be on her side.

BON COURAGE GISELLE!

The final preparations were checking through everything she was to take and wear in France. To be caught out by a small detail: an incorrect label or cigarette packet, would be disastrous and utterly preventable. Her blouse was allowed, as was her

KITTY TAYLOR by Sarah Colliver

lipstick, the gifts from Manon, which in her mind would be good luck charms.

"So, we will send home this envelope with the money, and your letter, in two weeks. Your parents are now aware that you are in the WAAF, which is good." Sylvia spoke faster than her usual measured way, and her hands busied themselves, when normally they were content to sit still on her desk or lap. She was on edge, Kitty thought. "So now, it's time to talk about your mission. Ready?"

Kitty inhaled a deep breath and acknowledged the range of emotions coursing through her body. She felt as though she needed to use the lavatory again, but she had already been twice. "Yes. Ready."

"You will be dropped into Fornay, where we need eyes on the ground. We need information about a factory we believe is developing a new type of bomb, but it is listed as a hospital. The circuit has been compromised in the surrounding areas, and we need to set them back up. You will work in the boulangerie, on Rue des Poissonniers, alongside Madame Valerie Aubert. You are her niece and have recently lost your husband; his estranged family disowned you when he died, and so

KITTY TAYLOR by Sarah Colliver

you have moved away to live with, and assist, Valerie. Your courier is Lucile Cheval, she is experienced and lived out there for many years before the war. That's the basics. Comprendre?"

"Oui Madame. I understand." Kitty absorbed every detail. Sylvia was fighting to disguise her slight lip quiver, but nothing escaped Kitty's notice.

"These are your papers, take a moment to familiarise yourself with them, where will you keep them? It needs to feel natural. We need you to take as much money as we can strap to you, as this is needed for bribes, and for the resistance to acquire explosives and weapons. We will also send a new wireless operator with you. They are desperate as the last one has gone MIA and, we suspect, may have been arrested. He will accompany you on the flight which, all being well, should take off at around 2200 hours tonight."

This was it. It was really happening. By tomorrow she would be wandering the streets of Fornay, and baking in a real French boulangerie. She would be fighting in the war. Her fingers felt for the delicate silver cross around her neck, given on her christening day. It had been Grand-mère's, then her mother's, and always

KITTY TAYLOR by Sarah Colliver

passed down to the eldest girl in the family. It would protect her. She kissed it and tucked it back under her green silk scarf.

"Do you have any questions? You know you can still back out, you don't have to do this." Syvia's solemn tone was sobering.

Every question Kitty thought of, she immediately answered herself. The training had been comprehensive and seemed to have covered everything. "So, six weeks is the plan for me to stay."

"Yes. That should give you enough time to gather the intel and stay relatively inconspicuous. Kitty, expect a little attention on arrival, you are a pretty girl and bound to turn heads. Use it to your advantage, play at a simpler version of yourself. Don't indicate just how capable you are…that way you can be visible without causing suspicion. You do understand?"

"It's like an acting role, really. Giselle is somebody else and from here on, I leave Kitty behind, for now at least."

KITTY TAYLOR by Sarah Colliver

"Good. Okay. Now, you should eat. It may feel like the last thing you want to do right now, but you must keep up your strength, you've a long 24 hours ahead of you."

The heavy rumble of the engines ricocheted through her, as her companion climbed up and slumped awkwardly opposite. The parachutes strapped to her back contorted her body into a strange angle and the tight straps constricted her breath. Yet, blood surged through her veins, and it felt as though she were awaking from a long sleep. Of course she was terrified, but she was excited too, with a feeling of invincibility. How many 23-year-old women, got a chance to fight like a man? 'Katarina, I'm coming with you too.' Grand-mère's voice played over in her head; she wasn't alone at all. She stared at the face of her fellow occupant, and realised she recognised him. Beneath his helmet and goggles, he looked white and clammy.

"Are you ok?" Kitty asked the wily man, Florin, who Dominique had taken a fancy to.

He nodded and squeezed his eyes shut.

KITTY TAYLOR by Sarah Colliver

"Nerves? Flying? Or the parachute jump, which lays ahead?" Kitty giggled and her companion reached over to his side and vomited into a bucket. What good was he likely to be if he couldn't even cope with the journey. "Something you ate perhaps?"

He stared but said nothing. Kitty reached for the water bottle she had taken to leave on the plane. "Here, sip this."

"Thanks." He took the bottle and drank, wetting his lips with his tongue. "It's the flying part if you must know. Used to be a pilot, haven't been on a plane…since…" He shook his head and took three deep sharp breaths. Colour flushed his face, and it was as though he had regained control of his body and mind. "Enough, we're not supposed to give anything away."

Kitty chewed her lip. That would teach her for judging, he had reason to hate flying and feel that way by the sounds of it. She needed to be more level-headed; less quick to jump to conclusions, but as soon as her self-doubt arrived, she swept it away, 'I am Giselle Lavigne, my husband has recently died. I am staying with my aunty to help in the shop…'

KITTY TAYLOR by Sarah Colliver

Kitty needn't have worried if her courage would fail when the time came, because one hard shove from her companion, ensured there was no backing out. She plunged towards the earth grappling for her cord, as she fought the urge to scream. Somewhere beneath lay her destiny, and her immediate fate. Could she make it to the ground without being spotted by the enemy? Would she be captured or instantly executed by a machine gun? Were her comrades ensuring her safety already? Questions sped through her mind as fast as she hurtled towards the earth. She yanked the parachute cord, and her descent slowed. A fusion of emotions flooded her, fear, exhilaration, excitement, and pain. It was more uncomfortable this time than the practice jump she completed back in the safety of home. Probably due to the wads of used bank notes strapped to her body, and extra clothing she had on. There would be no denying what her purpose was if she were to be captured on landing, and there would be no time to reach for her cyanide capsule. Fear threatened to take hold, but she shook it away, she needed her wits about her if she was going to survive the next few weeks.

KITTY TAYLOR by Sarah Colliver

The beacons of her landing party grew nearer; she steered herself as best as she could towards them, praying it was not a trap. Her jumbled mind fought to remember the drill for landing. The last thing she needed was an injury. For a split second she wondered where her companion was, but he would have to take care of himself, she must look after herself first.

She landed with a thud but avoided injury, as in training. Quickly and with muted gestures, Kitty was surrounded by a team of men and women, who helped fold her parachute and collect the items which were dropped separately alongside them. Her feet barely touched the ground as she was guided into the back of a delivery truck, followed in by two welcoming faces, both worn and tired. The whole arrival took only moments and was completed in relative silence.

"Welcome and thank you," the lady spoke in a whisper and the man offered a hip flask.

"Brandy?" He pushed the flask into her shaking hand.

"Merci." Kitty's dry lips stuck to her teeth, so she swilled a mouthful around to moisten them.

"Raymond and Lucile."

KITTY TAYLOR by Sarah Colliver

"Giselle." Kitty nodded and forced a quivering smiled on to her face.

Florin must have been taken separately in another direction as no other vehicle could be heard. She removed her helmet, goggles, and jumpsuit, which were hurriedly bundled into a sack.

"Will I do?" she asked as she straightened her hair and neck scarf.

"Oui, perfect and your accent is good too. You will stay locally for tonight, and tomorrow you will walk to town, and your new home."

"Merci Lucile, you are most kind."

For a moment, on opening her eyes, Kitty was unsure on her whereabouts. She heaved her body up, still weary from only a few hours broken sleep and listened. She was in the countryside judging by the peace and gentle birdsong. It was 0600 hours and a farm close by were busy taking the cows to the milking parlour. Her mouth was dry, and she needed to use the toilet and wash up, ready for the day ahead. Lucile was waiting outside as promised, sat on an old stone step. Kitty waved to her from the window and indicated she would be five minutes.

She poured the water from a tall floral jug into the matching wash bowl. With only two hours of fitful sleep, the icy water immediately revived her as she splashed her face.

"Salut, Giselle. You ready?" Lucile greeted her cheerfully, and Kitty wondered how she was so spritely on such little sleep.

Kitty nodded, wishing she had eaten more the night before, when Sylvia advised her to. Her nerves had prevented her from doing more than nibble on a little sliced bread. Her empty stomach groaned, and she couldn't decide if she was more hungry or tired.

"I will walk you to the edge of the trees, and you will continue alone to the checkpoint, at the bridge. You'll see the town from there. Just keep following the road, even when you get into town stay on it, and it will lead eventually to a large square. From there, you can pop into the Café Renaissance and ask for directions to the nearest fish shop. Your place is on the same street.

KITTY TAYLOR by Sarah Colliver

Only one boulangerie along there, Rue des Poissonniers. You got all of that?"

"Yes. I have this for you too. Here." Kitty handed over a large wedge of bank notes. "I was told you needed this."

Lucile pulled her into the thicket. "You cannot be too careful now, you don't know who is watching and anyone can inform on you. You must be more discreet," Lucile scolded Kitty.

"Sorry, it's the lack of sleep I think, or the hunger…"

Lucile shook her head. "You cannot afford to let either of those things affect you, you must be on guard Giselle. Now, give it to me." Lucile stuffed the money into the pocket of her rucksack. "You have your papers to hand? Everyone here has them easily accessible."

"They're in the inside pocket of my jacket."

"Okay, you have a gun? Give that to me and the rest of the money too, in case they search you. They often do that to anyone presenting as new to the area, at least, they are more likely to."

KITTY TAYLOR by Sarah Colliver

Kitty paused for a moment. The thought of giving her protection, and all the money to a stranger whom she had only just met...

"There is no time for that," Lucile said, as though reading her mind. "Trust me, when you're stood waiting at the checkpoint, you will be relieved that we have done this. I cannot afford for you to be arrested."

Kitty realised these decisions were going to crop up regularly, which would involve her choosing one action or another, and result in life or death. She emptied the money into Lucile's bag and then put in her pistol too.

"Okay, let's walk, it's about an hour from here to the checkpoint." Lucile was already heading away. "I will keep these at the barn, and when we rendezvous, you can have them back. Okay?"

Kitty nodded. "Will you contact me about where the barn is?"

"Let's just get you safely into Madame Aubert's, then we will make contact. A parcel will be left with her, containing a book, 'Grief and the darkness of loss,' which will be wrapped in brown paper. The coordinates will be stuck down underneath the spine, with when to come."

"Okay, I understand." Kitty smiled apprehensively as they strode closer towards the checkpoint, and her first encounter with the occupiers. Lucile turned back before it was visible, in the direction from where they came. Kitty was alone now.

The checkpoint was set up across the entrance to the majestical medieval bridge, which spanned the river. The uniforms and guns stained the otherwise perfect scene, which had inspired artists for hundreds of years. As she walked slowly towards the queue, she licked perspiration from her top lip, and wished her stomach would settle. The next five minutes could be the difference between life and death; torture even.

The two young guards were confident and jovial together, but their steely eyes narrowed towards the snaking line of people. This, her first encounter, face to face with the enemy, provoked deep fear that her papers were not realistic enough, if scrutinised, they would know. Her heart boomed and throat constricted as she fought to keep her nerves in check. She licked her lips and remembered the advice Sylvia had given

KITTY TAYLOR by Sarah Colliver

about the way she looked. She gathered her confidence, which at that moment was no more than a spark, lowered her head, so that her eyes looked coquettishly up at the young men. She stepped forward and held out her papers with a coy smile. The soldier narrowed his eyes as he checked her papers, "What is your business here, you aren't local?"

Kitty leaned in and lowered her voice, "My husband recently died; his family have sent me away. Can you imagine? I never liked them much anyway, and my father, he made me marry Alfonse. It's a fresh start." She shrugged her shoulders.

"I asked for your papers, not your life story." He glanced at her black arm band, worn to identify her to Madame Aubert on arrival, and to 'mourn her husband.' Then his eyes rested on her breasts, lingering for seconds longer than she was comfortable with. Facing the enemy at close range, a gun sat in his belt within touching distance, was a bleak reminder of how fragile life was every moment there. "On you go." He handed back her identification, and nodded her away, his cold eyes already focussed on the next person.

KITTY TAYLOR by Sarah Colliver

She crossed the bridge slowly, pausing for a moment to look upriver at the town nestled on the bank, and to catch her breath. It was going to be exhausting, keeping up a false persona every moment of every day, and this was only the beginning. Why had she thought she could manage this? But her papers had worked, and now she could work on blending in and hopefully make a difference. She swallowed away her doubts and stood tall as she marvelled at the beauty of the sweeping river and ancient town.

Rue des Poissonniers was only two streets from the main square. She had found it without the need to ask, by luck more than judgement. It was tucked away with the fish mongers at the end. There was little footfall apart from residents and shoppers, because it wasn't a cut through to anywhere. The boulangerie shop front was painted light blue, and the sign above expertly written in cursive writing. It reminded her of the blackboard at Manon's, back home.

A middle-aged lady, smartly dressed, with a cream apron tied at the front, stood leaning on the doorframe with her arms folded across her chest. Kitty nodded and smiled, adjusting her black armband.

KITTY TAYLOR by Sarah Colliver

"Giselle! Welcome! I was so sorry to hear about Alfonse. You must be devastated!" The lady pulled her into a tight embrace and kissed her on each cheek. "Come in! Come in!" She linked her arm and guided her in through the door. "Such good timing, as I was about to close."

Kitty stood and surveyed the empty shelves, only a few items remained.

"Closing so soon?" A small elderly lady with dark eyes pushed her way through the semi-closed door and stared at Kitty. "This is your…"

"Niece, Giselle. I told you about her coming to stay last week. Giselle, this is Madame Thomas. She lives over the street, has lived there her whole life!"

"So, you've travelled a long way by bus?" Her gruff voice matched her dark appearance.

"No, train first and then a bus to the other side of the bridge." In training they were taught to stick as close to the truth as possible, it gave an authenticity to the lie. "Just beyond the checkpoint." Kitty smiled. "I'm very tired, Aunty." She rested her head on Valerie's shoulder and rubbed her eyes.

KITTY TAYLOR by Sarah Colliver

"Will you excuse us please, I would like to properly welcome Giselle, and I am closing now anyway."

"I've come for my bread and while I'm here, I will say, your loaves aren't like they used to be, Madame."

"Of course they aren't, I cannot get the ingredients I used to make them with, I'm not a magician."

"Here," she slammed the coins on the counter. "It's the exact money and you are thief, stealing from a poor old woman."

"No one is forcing you to buy them, I can easily sell them to someone else." Valerie wrapped the loaves together, and held them for a moment, as if trying to decide whether she wanted to let them go.

"I've paid you now. Hand them over." Madame Thomas snatched them from Valerie and tucked them under her arm.

"Merci, au revoir!" Valerie ushered her out of the shop and bolted the door. She pulled down the blinds, reversed the open sign to closed, and took a deep breath. "That woman will be the death of me. Now, please, follow me."

KITTY TAYLOR by Sarah Colliver

Kitty followed Valerie out to the back of the shop and up a narrow flight of stairs to the living room and kitchen, one large room with dual aspect. "Please sit." She pulled a chair out for Kitty. "You can see that we have a watcher, she knows everything about everyone it seems. And so, we must always be careful, you understand?"

Kitty nodded and gratefully sipped the water placed in front of her on the table. She drained the glass.

"Please help yourself." Valerie pointed to the water carafe on the table, and Kitty poured another. "You must think of me as your aunt now. We must always behave like kin. It's so easy to forget and let it slip otherwise."

"I understand, Aunty." Kitty smiled, her eyes felt heavy and the last 36 hours finally seemed to have caught up with her.

"Let me show you to your room, it's small, but adequate. And I have tried to make it as comfortable as possible."

Another flight of stairs led up to a small landing with two doors. Kitty's room was at the back. The sloping ceilings created an awkward shape, but Valerie was right, it was more than adequate; it was 'cosy.' "Thank you."

"You look as though you are about to collapse. Why not try your bed and settle in. I will let you know when food is ready later."

"That sounds wonderful." Kitty was already perched on the edge of the bed removing her shoes. Her weary mind begged for respite. She slipped under the quilt and amidst the scent of lavender, from the small posy by her bed, drifted off into an exhaustive sleep.

BUSINESS AS USUAL

Kitty took the list which Valerie had written, and one of the larger baskets. It was a clever idea to use her provisions list to familiarise herself with the area, but also introduce herself, to alleviate any suspicious gossips. She had memorised the address and position on the map of the 'hospital' and would be passing near that way, enroute to the pharmacy. It was an easy

KITTY TAYLOR by Sarah Colliver

enough excuse to have 'lost her bearings' for going along the wrong road.

Narrower streets, lined with towering white, old buildings with rickety shutters, led off the main roads. It felt as though with every other turn of corner, a new square appeared, covered with trees and canopies, tables, and chairs. The sun beat down on her face, and she stood still for a moment, to enjoy the warmth on her skin. Life seemed to be carrying on as normal, which was difficult to understand, against the flutter of the scarlet flags emblazoned with swastikas. The enemy were everywhere, but the citizens had no choice but to forge on, because life must continue in some way. Babies would be born, shopping bought, and children still needed school. Kitty leant against the bark of a gnarly old tree and looked around.

It was not so different to home – a child screaming to be carried. A dog cocking his leg against a lamp post. A car horn honking aggressively at a lingering pedestrian in his way. She smiled. And then heavy thunderous boots, marching in time, followed a man shackled at his ankles and wrists. His face bloodied and swollen; Kitty thought he must be unrecognisable even to those he loved. A sign around his neck: TRAITOR. She blinked away her tears as she imagined Valerie in his place, and the danger which accommodating Kitty placed her in. She fought to push the thoughts from her mind.

She wanted to look away, she wanted to run, but she could not do that; maybe slip quietly away down a back street, without being noticed? But soldiers now enclosed the square, to ensure this spectacle was witnessed by as many as possible. They even made the shopkeepers come and stand in front of their shops.

The gathering crowd stood in groups; hands reached out for comfort and eyes stared at the pavement, too frightened to watch the horror unfolding. The largest tree in the centre of the once bustling and joyful square, was now the focal point. What events it must have absorbed over centuries, sights it had seen and changes it witnessed. Now, reduced to a sinister executioners assistant, complicit to murder. They prodded the poor prisoner until he stood with his back against the tree; his bound hands gripped the twisted bark behind him.

"This is what you people can expect if you assist or have contact with the enemy. We will find you and we will kill you and your family." The clipped German shouted

KITTY TAYLOR by Sarah Colliver

in broken French, good enough to make himself understood.

Kitty scowled but quickly brought her face back to a blank stare, aware of the precarious situation she had found herself in, simply by walking around the town.

The German nodded to a subordinate, who slowly stepped nearer to the man, his pistol aimed at his forehead. In a final moment of defiance, the prisoner straightened up, puffed out his chest and shouted, "Liberte!"

How brave, Kitty thought as she wiped tears from her eyes.

The double shot echoed around the square and his blood sprayed anyone close by to the tree. The crowd gasped, and a woman wailed. The soldiers regrouped and marched away, leaving his lifeless body and mess all around. The square, now stained crimson with fresh blood, began to empty as the crowd dispersed slowly. Kitty could not move, she was rigid with fear, despair, and horror. The square was now still; devoid of life, as the shopkeepers returned to their shops and shoppers escaped the bloody scene, their stomachs no longer hungry. Kitty wanted to move the poor man, give him a scraping of dignity among his cruel death. But where to, and should she help clear up? If she behaved out of the ordinary, she could be noticed, and she must fade into the background. There was so much more she needed to do, and she couldn't take risks by being seen as anything more than a silent bystander. So, she left, like the others, walked away, to continue her daily business, as though she hadn't witnessed an execution. What choice did she have? Life continued around the insane and violent actions of the occupiers.

Two left turns, and a ten-minute walk along an avenue of trees and brasseries, took her to a large building with a Hospital sign. Everything about it looked like a medical building. The parked ambulances, the façade of the old grand building. But Kitty noticed a lack of patients, and there were buses parked around the back, and the hint of a large tunnel could be seen behind. She needed to get inside, to see if it was being used as a hospital at all. Once she had found her feet, she could dig around a little, see if anyone had been treated there. But she couldn't risk looking too curious for now. She would have to wait. And if all else failed, perhaps she would sustain an injury herself, see where she would be taken.

Now she was familiar with the barn, the book having been delivered two days after arrival, she could get messages to and from London via Lucile. Lucile, in turn, passed information to Florin who radioed London. This level of separation was vital, in case of arrest and interrogation – you cannot give locations of people if you don't know where they are. Kitty had no idea where Florin operated from, or where Lucile and Raymond lived. The only place she knew, was their meeting place of the barn. Although she had destroyed the message, the book was a useful prop to carry around, adding an authenticity to her story, as a grieving widow. If she needed to survey a street or area, she could pose as a 'reader' on a bench or step. She would ask for an update from the others about the hospital, when they next met.

KITTY TAYLOR by Sarah Colliver

TRUST YOUR INSTINCT

"Your technique is excellent; you've been well taught!" Valerie sipped her early morning coffee and watched Kitty knead the latest batch of dough.

"Merci, I have always baked with my family, since I was little."

"It shows, you look experienced. You know, it's good having company here, sharing the work. I'm glad you came, Cherie."

Kitty stopped kneading and stared at Valerie.

"Giselle, are you ok? You look like you've seen a ghost! Is it because I called you Cherie? Do you mind?"

Kitty couldn't decide if she should object, it being a pet name belonging to Kitty, rather than Giselle, or take it as a lucky sign. Perhaps it was a bridge between her two personas, and it implied a close relationship, which seemed to be developing quickly and naturally.

"I don't mind. I like it." Kitty smiled and continued with her bread. She was enjoying their early morning preparation chats, as the world awoke to a new day. They never talked about why Kitty was there, or what she was up to. It was 'brushed under the carpet' and they settled into their pretend roles. Valerie asked no questions, and Kitty offered no information, but Kitty knew that Valerie lay awake worrying, waiting for her to return. And that she held back her fears each time she left the shop, just as Kitty prevented her mind from imagining what would happen to Valerie should Kitty be caught. You couldn't live under the same roof and not care.

"I won't be in for supper tonight. I'm not sure when I'll be back."

Valerie nodded. "I'll save it, for whenever you return. Oui?"

"Merci." Kitty smiled.

"Perhaps you should have a little nap this afternoon, so you are refreshed for whatever later entails. A clear mind is safer you know." Valerie nodded her head and sipped the last of her coffee.

Kitty was surprised how quickly their bond was developing, and it made her reflect on her own mother. Their relationship was tepid and strained; the opposite of how she and Valerie were already interacting. An immediate ease sat between them, which Kitty was grateful for. Living with such uncertainty and constant danger took its toll. Having someone who you did not have to explain to or pretend with, offered a little respite in an otherwise overwhelming situation.

It seemed true what they say, you can't choose your family. Kitty always felt like the 'accident', like a sordid secret, having been conceived out of wedlock. The words she once overheard in a heated exchange between her mother and Grand-mère, when her mother declared that falling pregnant had caused her to be shunned and whispered about in the street. Before they left France Celeste was branded as 'loose' and that her child would be a bastard, and this always made Kitty resent her mother for being so reckless in forever causing Kitty to feel ashamed.

Strange though, how she felt strangely at peace with leaving Grand-mère. Perhaps because she was in France and it felt as though that connected them together. She was sure that she was ever-present, as Kitty's protector.

A drop was planned for the evening, and Kitty was apprehensive, the knot in her stomach told her so.

KITTY TAYLOR by Sarah Colliver

Something felt strange about it, was it instinct gnawing away at her? Should she call it off? Or could it be down to the fact that everything carried so much weight, with the enemy all around. Even in the boulangerie, she eyed every customer with caution, wondering if they were informants. She still conveyed a warm smile and friendly greeting, despite her suspicions.

It was difficult making the adjustment to her life, now immersed in an occupied zone. Back home, the fear was mainly from the sky and the havoc caused by the bombing raids, and for loved ones serving abroad. It was different in France. Fear was in every moment of the day, in every interaction and connection. The enemy in uniform was chilling but obvious, you KNEW who they were and where they stood. Those hiding in plain sight, dressed as civilians and living quietly, surveying and reporting, caused everyone to live in a permanent state of anxiety. That was exhausting in itself.

Kitty wiped her hands on a tea towel and sipped her water. It was more complicated out in the field than she ever imagined. There were so many things to consider all at once. So many 'what ifs.' She couldn't even take solace in smoking, as now it was prohibited for women to smoke, which made her more edgy. Smoking was good for her nerves, but she was relying solely on the pity of her male colleagues to supply her with measly rations, to smoke in privacy. She had one left, in the little glass dish in her room, for emergencies. "I'm going upstairs for a moment, do you mind? This is all done now, so it's over to you."

"Go, Cherie. I'll take over now." Valerie squeezed her arm and smiled.

Kitty edged away, as her mind fought to arrange her thoughts into order, she must have a clear head by the evening. She rubbed her forehead, hoping the threatening headache would come to nothing.

It was at least a ten-minute drive to the arranged drop point, from where they agreed to meet. Kitty chewed at her fingernail as she lent on a tree, furiously checking her watch. If they didn't hurry, they wouldn't make it in time. A distant car engine grew nearer, and she hid behind the tree, to check it was her comrades. The car stopped but the engine ran on.

KITTY TAYLOR by Sarah Colliver

"You're cutting it fine!" Kitty whispered as she jumped into the back.

"There was a roadblock, so we had to come the long way around."

"Let's hope that's the only spanner in the works tonight, and that we get this done smoothly." Kitty looked at each of them in turn. "Where's Philippe?"

"He didn't come. Lying low for a while, to work out if he's being tailed- he didn't want to lead anyone to us," Lucile replied.

"And you didn't think to get a message to me? That this is important enough to think about a re-sched?" Kitty's face flushed and her breath quickened. This was feeling worse by the moment. "Turn the car around, take us back to the barn!"

"You're crazy! We need this drop!" Raymond spat out his words and drove on.

"I said, turn the car around! We need to stop this now! If there are no beacons, then the plane returns to Britain. But if we go ahead, light them, guide them in, we could be leading them into a trap. And we could all die. I have a bad feeling about this."

"Giselle! You can't act on a bad feeling. Shit! I wouldn't do anything if I did." Raymond sounded as livid as Kitty felt.

"Do it. Turn around, before it's too late." She had already decided to grab the wheel if he didn't comply. Raymond turned the wheel and spun the car around.

"You crazy fucking woman. When we get back, we're having this out."

"Yes, we are." Kitty sat back in her seat and folded her arms to steady them. Her gut feeling about the drop, still evident in her constant need to urinate, refused to dissipate. Lucile was staring at Kitty, but turned her head away, in protest, and gazed out of the window as soon as Kitty looked at her. The atmosphere was heavy, weighted by frustration on all sides.

Raymond drove straight in through the open barn doors, jumped out of the car and pushed them closed behind them. "What the fuck was that?" he yelled, storming towards Kitty, his face scarlet and his fists clenched.

KITTY TAYLOR by Sarah Colliver

"It wasn't safe," Kitty slammed the car door shut. "If Philippe is being tailed, they may know about tonight, how much do we know about Philippe? Isn't it a bit suspect to back out last minute of a drop? Sounds fishy to me."

"So now you accuse Philippe of being a traitor? How much do we know about you Giselle? Nothing. Philippe has lived around us his whole life! How dare you say such things."

"You need to calm down, and stop shouting, both of you." Lucile stood between them, her outstretched arms keeping them apart. "Do you want the whole of France to hear you, because if they weren't alerted to us, they will be if this goes on much longer!"

Kitty huffed and turned away, fighting her nerves and questioning her own gut instinct. Raymond poured a red wine from a stash behind a crate of empty milk bottles and muttered under his breath, "this is crazy."

The problem was, when preparing for something like a drop, it was all consuming. The adrenaline rocketed and carried you through the fear. Suddenly that had nowhere to go, and they were directing it towards each other, Kitty understood. "You know, I could be wrong, maybe it would have been fine to carry on. But imagine, for a second, if I was right, my instinct correct; then I have just saved us all, and many more who we can go on to help. I think we must listen to our gut instincts, sometimes that's all we have!"

Lucile was coming round; Kitty could tell by the sympathetic look in her eye. Raymond, not so easy to convince, offered Lucile a cigarette. Pride prevented Kitty from moaning, which was what he wanted; for her to beg.

"So, tell me more about what's going on with Phillippe?" Kitty pulled a straw bale over and sat down.

Lucile joined her and passed the cigarette to her for a drag.

"He got a message to me, it was short and only said that he felt he may be being tailed and, until he could know for sure, he would lay low."

"So how do we know he wasn't tailed leaving the message? What if they followed him and then you?" Kitty battled with the panic which edged across her like

KITTY TAYLOR by Sarah Colliver

a dark shadow. What if they were being watched right now?

"He was extra careful, and used a phone box to call a contact, who left the message."

Kitty picked at a hole in her jacket, which was expanding like a nasty flesh-eating disease, and hoped she would remember to stitch it up before she wore it again. "We must all be extra vigilant, take no chances. If something feels off, listen to your feeling."

"Since when were you in charge anyway?" Raymond stared defiantly.

"She, like me, chose to come over here, to help. We didn't have to. Don't we deserve respect for that, at least?" Lucile smiled as she posed the question to Raymond. Kitty thought she looked like a film star in that moment, with her hair piled into a bandana and her high arched eyebrows.

"Any news on the 'hospital' yet? I'm trying to get there to take photographs, but I can't get anywhere near it without being noticed, too many Germans around," Kitty sighed.

"Still working on getting inside. My first contact let me down, but I will update you as soon as I hear." Raymond's tone was calmer and more amiable, but his eyes still narrowed towards her.

"Good. Right, time to go. Anything else?" Kitty stood up.

"I will drop you near town, if you like?"

"At the tree will do, my bike is there. Thanks." Kitty wasn't looking forward to the cycle home, but at least the bright moon could light her way. She crossed her fingers she would avoid being caught out after curfew.

EXPECT THE UNEXPECTED

Kitty couldn't sleep, but she was beyond exhausted. Every time she climbed into her warm cosy bed, she hoped to fall into a deep slumber, but her vivid thoughts plagued her: capture, torture, and the fear that perhaps they were being watched. She still had no proof, but it was as if her body was on high alert. It was like someone was sending her a message telepathically

KITTY TAYLOR by Sarah Colliver

and was as clear as a transmission on a radio. She couldn't shrug it off, but how do you convince strongminded, reactive people, to listen to your hunch? Raymond was doubting of her ability anyway, why should he listen to a woman? She was sure he wasn't being as careful as he should be. London was proving impatient, and in her mind, had little idea how tough it was facing the enemy whilst queuing for milk daily. They didn't have to swerve to avoid eye contact with Germans, or bat away the unwanted advances and wolf-whistles of virile young soldiers. London wanted a job done and seemed oblivious to the added complications, which prevented this and meant it would take longer. This disappointed her, and she couldn't fight the resentment which seeped in towards them.

Kitty had always noticed things in life, more than the average person going about their busy day. It was as though she saw life through a magnified camera lens, which flagged up detail or things that didn't sit right. She always thought it was a gift, but lately it was feeling all too much. Every agent in the field had to adapt to heightened perception to stay alive, hers felt multiplied by a thousand, with her mind working overtime. That's

KITTY TAYLOR by Sarah Colliver

why sleep evaded her. She absorbed too much information and then could not switch off from processing the 'what could happens.'

The ornate, wooden wall clock ticked loudly in her cosy petite room. It was 0300 hours, and there was little chance of sleep, she would tiptoe down the creaky stairs and make coffee. Wait for the sun to rise.

"Cherie, you too huh?" Valerie looked pasty and worn out, as she clasped her cup of coffee. "Come and sit with me, there's enough for you, and it's not long made."

Kitty sat down at the little round kitchen table and pulled her faded robe tight across her body. It was thoughtfully left hanging in her bedroom when she arrived, by Valerie. It was these small gestures of quiet kindness which endeared Valerie to her. Aside from the fact she was risking her life, allowing her to stay in the first place. "What keeps you awake?"

"Me? Where to begin, Cherie. War. Death. Snooping neighbours who make me sick to my core, who would inform on their own townsfolk for money. That's only the start..."

KITTY TAYLOR by Sarah Colliver

Kitty poured a coffee and topped up Valerie's too.

Valerie tucked a strand of Kitty's hair gently behind her ear. "I couldn't have children; we tried for many years. But it wasn't meant to be, and now I know I am glad of it, because I cannot imagine sending a son off to war. Or allowing a daughter to do this. Do your parents know, Cherie?"

"I'm sorry. That's so sad, but I do understand what you mean about it, this war is breaking the hearts of parents all over the world." She evaded Valerie's question. "What about your husband?"

"Cancer. Before the war. Fought his own battle. He was a good man."

Kitty held back her own tears, as she envisioned Grand-mère laying still, taking her last breath. "You've been alone, since then?"

"I've had a string of admirers, but no-one special. It's for the company more than anything. A childless widow gets used to pity stares and sympathy and that's not how I want to be seen. I am doing okay with my business; my life is comfortable."

KITTY TAYLOR by Sarah Colliver

"You have a lovely home." Kitty looked around at the variety of plants adorning the shelves, and framed artwork in varying sizes. A small stove burner, sat beneath a wooden mantle which was crammed with nicknacks and treasures. It was a cosy space, it felt alive. "You have a love of houseplants?"

"I got that from my father-he was a keen horticulturist. Taught me a few things. I must say, they cheer me up, bring the place to life, when it's only me here."

"Are you scared? About me being here?"

Valerie stood up and pulled a battered tin from the shelf. It was decorated with a painted cow stood next to a pail of milk, and had an ill-fitting lid. She pulled out two cigarettes and smiled. "From one of my admirers, they have their uses! Here, take one."

Kitty took it and laughed at how excited one cigarette could make her. Never would she have believed it before feeling the restrictions of the occupiers. They sat for a moment; the only sound was the inhalation and expelling of the smoke, which plumed into the air. It was a moment of easy calm, one to relish, one that was rare.

KITTY TAYLOR by Sarah Colliver

"I would be lying to say I wasn't scared, but we cannot sit back and allow them to take our country, tell us what we can and can't do. Kill us for nothing. Doesn't it make us as bad as them if we do nothing?"

"Your admirers, do you still see them?"

"Never here. Too many prying eyes, and Giselle, you don't have to worry, we never talk about our private lives. Just small talk. They know 'my niece' is visiting of course. and that's the perfect excuse not to spend too much time with them. To be honest I don't feel the need at the moment, when I have such wonderful company with you. For the record, I'm only close with one of them. You understand? I would hate you to think badly of me. We must be discreet, because word travels fast around here, and I would be labelled brazen." Valerie shrugged her shoulders.

"I would never think that of you. I think you're marvellous. Running your own boulangerie, being your own woman. It can't be easy." Kitty yawned. "God, I have to be up in two hours. Got an early mee…" She caught her words and sighed. How easy it would be to slip into over sharing. "Thanks Valerie, for all you do for me, you go above and beyond, and I cannot thank you enough."

Valerie nodded and squeezed her hand. "Take care today, I worry when you go out. Come home safely." She kissed her forehead and cleared away their cups.

Kitty straightened her skirt and pinned back her hair. Valerie had left a bottle green beret on the end of her bed, it was second hand, but perfect to compliment Kitty's complexion. Kitty adjusted it on her head, and told herself it would bring luck. She was meeting with a new contact, Henri. From the report she had been given, he narrowly escaped the Gestapo and was forced away from the area. Henri was not in a good way and his frayed nerves could result in carelessness. Sometimes, when agents were out in the field for too long, they cracked. She was meeting him to assess and arrange for him to be sent back to England. She had a safe house lined up where he could lay low until she got the details from HQ. They were still aggressively pressing for intel on the hospital, but this was adding to her growing frustration, and for the first time she could understand why agents cracked up. The pressure was suffocating, and she could only do so much. If it was as easy as wandering in and snapping photographs, then this would have been completed months ago. Maybe the injury idea, to see if she was treated at the hospital, was the only way after all, at least to get a foot in the door of the façade. But then she would be left with an injury, which put her more at risk.

She took her lipstick from the trinket dish on her bedside table, and carefully applied it, whilst Manon's voice reminded her, "we must keep up our standards." A tear rolled down her cheek, but she shook the sadness away, it would only cloud her thoughts.

She cycled faster than normal, breaking out in a sweat. Although she had left in plenty of time, she realised halfway there, that she had forgotten her handbag, with her papers, so doubled back to collect it. Her aching legs did not thank her carelessness, but it wasn't worth being stopped without her identification. The soldiers didn't need an excuse to terrorise anyone, so you made sure you didn't give them one either. She had seen a man shot at a checkpoint. For whatever their reason, they bolted at the last minute and were gunned down. A little boy in front of Kitty clutched his mother's skirt as she held his face away, amid his sobs. This was everyday life. It was exhausting.

She leaned her bicycle against a crumbling wall and took a moment to breath and check the time. By a miracle, she was only five minutes late, and that was nothing. The café was on the outskirts of town, the very last one before the forest outstretched towards the next village. It was quieter there; the owners were sympathetic to the partisans and opened early for locals to breakfast, before work. It would take a few minutes to wander there, and enough time to clear her head. The streets on the edge of town were mainly houses and she could hear the morning chatter of parents cajoling children to eat breakfast and get ready for school. It must be the same sounds the world over.

A distant car screeching to a halt, followed by a second maybe two streets away, stopped Kitty in her tracks. It was in the direction of where she was headed. Shouting and car doors slamming echoed and penetrated her core. Fear crept along her skin, and she wondered if this was the way she would be captured.

Kitty pressed herself into the nook of the wall and prayed she hadn't been spotted. Someone must have given away the location of their meet. Her heart pounded and she slowly edged away from the corner in the direction of her recently abandoned bicycle, keeping her eyes focused on the unfolding scene just out of sight. A hand clasped over her mouth and muffled her screams.

"Shh. Don't make a fuss, I'm going to help you." The whisper reminded her of her interrogation training and her mind fought to think up a quick plan. She would comply and as soon as her captor thought she was under control, she would run away, one way or another. She allowed him to steer her down into a dark cobbled courtyard, surrounded by boarded up windows, surveying the area for possible routes of escape.

"Don't you recognise me?"

The voice was familiar… He stepped away from her, and into a stream of light, which cut through the shadows from behind a small break in the roof. Kitty gasped.

"Oh my God!" Her brain fought to process what this even meant.

KITTY TAYLOR by Sarah Colliver

"Why are you here? It's too dangerous?" His voice was full of concern, and she was impressed with his accent, not having communicated in French with him before. "They should not have sent you out here!"

Kitty's nostrils flared and in a shouty whisper she threw her words at him, "I could ask the same of you! Why is it okay for you to be here and not me?"

"You're not a soldier! You work in the Café de Flore on Solomon Street. That's what I think about, while enduring all this: you, safe, making your delicious soup and smiling that damn seductive smile of yours. And now, you're HERE? Do you have any idea what you have got yourself involved with?" He clutched her arms tightly. "This is crazy..." He pulled her into his chest and kissed her deeply. Desire burned through Kitty's body. The war-damaged surroundings faded around them.

"Go to this address, 4, Rue de la Fontaine, it has a green door." He squeezed her hand and brushed his lips over each of her fingers. "I will follow you, make sure we aren't being watched. We can talk there."

Kitty knew what he meant by 'talking', maybe they would talk afterwards, but she had seen those brown eyes full of lust many times. She kissed him again and then pulled away towards the street, marvelling at what had unfolded. How many times recently had she wished for a friendly face, somebody she could trust? But never, ever, could she have imagined that Sebastian would appear. She thought back to when she saw him last with his tan, which he could not have got in Britain. It made sense, all the sudden appearances and departures, and how little she knew about him.

As she reached the green door, she checked all around, whilst 'tying up her shoelace' and Sebastian arrived swiftly, opening it enough for them to move inside. She was barely through the door when he pushed her hard against the wall, pinning her with the weight of his strong body. His lips, not quite close enough to kiss, moved as he whispered, "I can't believe you're here!" He gently kissed her lips. "Is this actually happening?"

Her legs threatened to buckle at his voice, his touch, his warm breath on her face. Her fingers twisted into his thick brown hair and pulled his head to hers. Her lips hungrily kissed him; she wanted to devour him. All the stress and struggles of the last few weeks melted into animal instinct, as she pulled at his clothes and threw them to the ground. She trailed her hands over the muscles of his torso, he was slimmer than before but more golden, and she peppered his taut skin with kisses, as he fought to remove the last of her underwear. Fuelled by her groans of pleasure, he moved fast and furiously, with pure abandonment, as though it was their last moments on earth. Kitty eagerly grasped at his firm buttocks, desperate for more, throwing back her head and submitting to his full control in the moment. His mouth kissed her neck, breasts and all the skin in between, whilst his hands firmly pushed her harder to him. This was exactly what she needed, a release from everything she had endured.

Kitty awoke and rubbed sleep from her eyes. Sebastian stood silhouetted in the window, his naked frame like a renaissance painting. She gasped at his beauty. "What time is it?" The light gave nothing away.

"Four." He turned and smiled. "You were tired! Cigarette?" She nodded and he lit one, handing it to her "I'm not surprised, I think it was the 'making up for lost time'- it wore you out!"

Kitty yawned and propped herself up with a pillow. The room was nice, much larger than hers with lofty ceilings and fancy wall sconces. It even had a bathroom. "Reality is, we shouldn't be here, like this, should we?"

"I won't tell if you don't." He climbed back into the bed and pulled a sheet up over his stomach. "We're only human, don't we deserve a little down time?" He sighed. "It's so intense here and, well, what we did; I feel like a new man."

Kitty smiled. They were good together. But he knew who she really was. No one else in France did. It complicated everything. She was behaving like Kitty, and she needed to be wholly Giselle. This put her in danger. She cursed herself; it had all happened so quickly and unexpectedly. If she had been able to think clearly about it, the situation, she would surely have declined, no matter how much her stomach fluttered at the thought of it. Should she tell him her code name, to stop him using Kitty? Should she ask him questions about what he was doing there? All of her training and instincts told her to say nothing, ask nothing.

"When did you get here? How have we not bumped into each other sooner?" He smiled and tilted his head slightly.

KITTY TAYLOR by Sarah Colliver

"A while ago." She inhaled the cigarette.

"Where you staying?"

Kitty pondered the question. "Not too far from here."

"Wow. You aren't giving much away. It's only me for God's sake." He traced his fingers around her nipple which immediately hardened with his touch. "I've missed these, such beautiful breasts..."

She smacked away his hand, suddenly repelled by the situation "Have you got any food? I'm starving." Her appetite had shifted from the carnal to carnivore and she wished for a plate of ham and cheese.

Sebastian stood and dressed. "I can sort that out for you, I'll be right back mademoiselle." He took her hand and kissed it, doffed his pretend hat, and left.

Kitty stubbed out her cigarette in the ashtray; already five ends deep, and took her clothes from the heap on a chair in the corner, to dress. Her bag hung on a hook above next to Sebastian's jacket and pulling it into her face she inhaled his citrus, smoky scent. Why was this happening? What brought them together now? What did it all mean? She slipped her hand into the jacket pockets, but found only loose coins and a handkerchief, and a sense of guilt for snooping. She wasn't even sure what she was looking for, or why. She pulled out an open pack of cigarettes and popped them into her handbag.

Her hair was a mess, so she pinned it back into place, and pulled on her beret, which made her look immediately more presentable. She surveyed the room. The ceiling to floor window, with the Juliette balcony, overlooked the square. It was the perfect spot for people watching. Sebastian was on his way back, passing the fountain. She stepped back to avoid being seen and sat on the velvet chair, which her clothes had previously covered. She would eat and then leave. Valerie would be worried, as she left before 7am. She must consider this latest development with Sebastian too - their meeting could jeopardise so many brave souls involved in their circuits. It wasn't only about the two of them. One false move, and it was over for them all, and for what? Sex. Anger rose up inside her as quickly as the desire had previously. How could she have allowed this to escalate? Her hunger pangs dissipated, and the walls felt as though they were closing in on her. She grabbed her bag and tied up her laces.

Henri. Probably being tortured at this very moment. How could she have been so distracted from this; how could the strength of her desire overpower her ability to think clearly? The room spun and she felt out of control, and furious that she allowed this to happen. She must get a message to London. The only good thing was that Henri knew nothing about their circuit, because their meet had not happened, thank God she had forgotten her papers and was late arriving.

"Oh. You're leaving?" Sebastian's confused face crumpled in surprise.

"This isn't right. Not here and now. You know this too." Kitty's arms flayed in frustration, as she fought to keep control.

Sebastian placed his bag on the dressing table and grabbed her arms. "Surely, we must take what comforts we can in these dark times. What's wrong with that?"

Kitty shook her head and pulled her arms free of his firm grasp. "You really believe that? Look, I don't want any information about why you are here, and I don't expect you to ask me anything either. But I can guess your reason is similar to mine, and the fact that we know each other makes this even more risky. We both must stay alert; aware of everything going on around us, down to the minutest detail. People's safety depends on us."

"Well, how about we forget who we were, and stick to who we are now. Sebastian is sat in England drinking coffee with Kitty. I, on the other hand, am Michel Bernard." He held out his hand as though they were meeting for the first time.

Kitty's hands flew to her ears, and she spun away from him, "No! You're saying too much. I need to think. We know too much…I'm sorry. None of this should have happened, you caught me by surprise, that's all. Goodbye Sebastian." She pushed past him, through the door, and down the stairs, fighting back tears which threatened to choke her. She had let everyone down, and all the while, Henri was at the hands of the Gestapo.

KITTY TAYLOR by Sarah Colliver

UPSIDE DOWN

Kitty paced in a figure of eight, scowling. Henri was in the hands of the Gestapo, and she felt sick thinking about what he may be enduring. There was no way she could help him, but perhaps he was able to reach his cyanide capsule and would have a more peaceful end than what else was on offer. Her own capsule was always close by, having had London put in a tiny, concealed pocket in her bra.

Her brain felt full and messy, but at least London was aware of his capture. She organised that as soon as she left Sebastian, using the emergency drop location for her message. In usual circumstances, Kitty went through Lucile, but there were different rules in case of emergencies. The view at the edge of the forest was of the meandering river far below, leading towards the town. From this distance, one could be fooled into believing life was normal. She chewed at her nail until it bled and winced with the pain.

She picked up her bicycle and headed off towards the barn. She was due to meet Raymond and Lucile and would fill them in with the Henri situation, yet she pondered for a moment. What if one of *them* had been

KITTY TAYLOR by Sarah Colliver

the betrayer? Perhaps they had warned the Gestapo of the meeting? Impossible, she hadn't told them the location or time. This made her feel a little better and settled the somersaults of fear in her stomach. No, she had no reason to doubt either of them. She hid her bike in the thick undergrowth five minutes from the barn, and checked she wasn't being followed before heading over and knocking on the weathered door.

"Giselle. You're as white as a sheet." Lucile opened the door and pulled her in. Kitty suspected that she and Raymond were an item, but it was only a guess based on minute gestures they shared, which to anyone else would probably go unnoticed.

Raymond continued to study the map spread out across the solid old table and spoke without looking up. "Okay?"

"My meeting was intercepted. Henri was arrested."

Raymond stood; his eyebrows raised.

"I was running late, forgot my ID, so only five minutes or so, but as I got close by, I heard the cars, and saw the commotion. I didn't hang around in case they saw me. If I'd arrived on time…"

KITTY TAYLOR by Sarah Colliver

"But you didn't. You're here."

"Lucky for us he didn't have any information on this section. All he knew was to meet a contact, so he can tell them nothing. He got his orders direct from London just before his radio operator left for England. Thank God. At least that means minimal damage."

"Thank God? Do you know what they will do to him?" Raymond's puce face contorted into a tight accusatory pose. "What they are probably doing to him now? Don't thank your God because where is he?"

Kitty slumped onto a bale of hay, she had no answer, but also the feeling that he had more to say and needed to vent.

"If there was a God, how would he allow what those monsters are doing? The murdering, their insatiable appetite for torture? I don't think I want that kind of God…"

Lucile touched his arm, but he shrugged her away.

"I don't disagree, and I didn't mean it the way it sounded." Kitty could not deny her insensitive comment. "But it does mean for now, anyway, we are safe. But we must take extra precautions, double check for tails, and anything unusual we need to discuss. And for the record, I can't bear to think about what Henri may be enduring, but I must concentrate on what we *can* do. What safety measures to put in place, to prevent the same happening to us. I still have my orders to complete; I didn't come here to enjoy the scenery…"

"I agree," Lucile replied and Raymond nodded reluctantly. "Does London know?"

"Yes, I used the emergency drop." Kitty scratched her head and sighed. "I've been thinking about the hospital too. The only way I'm going to get anywhere near the hospital is to sustain an injury. It needs to be bad enough to need hospital treatment but not life changing…any ideas?"

Raymond laughed, "You really are crazy."

"From what I've seen, it's no hospital, has anyone you know ever been there for treatment? But I don't think that is enough proof for London. I need evidence. I'm going to start with photographs of the outside, the buses, and if I can, the tunnel, slightly visible behind. But I really need to get inside to confirm it."

"Trouble is, it's crawling with Germans along that stretch, they all use the cafes and bars. We need to see when the quietest time of day is. I have a contact who has recently started working in one of those, I will ask him." Lucile smiled. She was always so helpful and supportive.

"Is he safe?" Kitty frowned, her mistrust of other humans growing daily.

"Sure. Without telling you too much, he is a contact of Florin. He may even be able to help with photos of the exterior."

Kitty nodded, "Well, don't say too much, I'm feeling twitchy at the moment."

Raymond sniggered. "Another of your hunches?"

"London absolutely agreed shutting down the drop was the right thing to do. They haven't got an endless line of volunteers waiting and trained to come here you know. It takes time, resources, and the correct kind of idiot, to be parachuted into occupied territory."

KITTY TAYLOR by Sarah Colliver

Raymond's face softened as he continued to stare at her. It was as though he suddenly remembered she had *chosen* to put herself into the same constant, imminent danger they all faced. "Well, we all lived another day because of it, so I suppose that's a victory, not failure."

Kitty swayed at this new development and smiled. Perhaps they had turned a corner, and he finally accepted they were on the same side.

"I think that a fractured finger may be the least impactful injury. Would need attention, and if you did it on your... wait, you are right-handed, yes?" Raymond asked.

Kitty nodded.

"Then we break your left. One or two?"

Kitty winced at the thought, and wondered if she would lose this newfound respect if she backed out...

"No time like the present. I suggest that we do it here, then you head up near the hospital, and stage a fall. The closest place for treatment will be there. Your injury is the easy part, drawing the attention of the surrounding Germans, that's the unnerving part. Up for it?"

Kitty took a deep breath, it was out of her control now, but if it worked, it may be the best idea she ever had.

Her hand throbbed, and tiny beads of sweat bled from the pores on her face. She could feel her fingers swelling and dreaded how she was going to fall without inflicting more damage, but ensuring it looked convincing. Raymond had offered to go with her, but she refused, not wanting them to be seen together. She fought her guilt towards Valerie, who would by now be worried sick about her, but reasoned that she was only in France to do her job, and Valerie was not her priority. Bile burned in her throat. Lucile had carefully applied lipstick to Kitty's paled mouth before she left, and they had dropped her on the outskirts of town, as she could not ride her bicycle. The boulevard lined with trees, was beginning to fill up with people seeking dinner, and she silently snarled at a glamourous French women cosied up to a German officer, enjoying his intent interest and his wallet. Perhaps she would try and steal his attention; that would teach the traitorous whore. She headed towards the pavement where their table sat, and his wandering eye focussed on her, as her foot

KITTY TAYLOR by Sarah Colliver

'slipped off the kerb' and she fell to the floor with a whelp.

Her eyes stung with tears of pain, and she felt the colour drain from her face. She lay awkwardly on the road, hoping she wouldn't be hit by a passing car.

"Please, may I?" His French accent was good. She looked up as he knelt beside her and began to examine for injury. "Where does it hurt mademoiselle?"

"My hand," Kitty replied in a small voice, extending her hand and two misshapen fingers.

"Anywhere else, before I move you from the road?"

"I don't think so, my hand - I'm in a lot of pain, but I don't want to be any bother, please help me up and I can be on my way." She raised her eyes to his, as though imploring his help.

"Frederick, come back to the table, she can manage. She said so." A gloved hand squeezed his shoulder.

"This woman is injured! What does that make me if I ignore her, when she lays on the road right in front of me? Please go back and enjoy the wine. I will take her to get treatment and then return."

KITTY TAYLOR by Sarah Colliver

His trollop scowled at Kitty, and without saying a word, sat back at the little bistro table under the burgundy canopy.

The Officer helped Kitty to her feet. "You look as though you might faint, are you sure you can stand, ok?"

"I think so." She wasn't acting, the pain was real.

"How fortunate we are to be so close to the hospital. Allow me to take you." He gently moved her injured hand across her chest to her opposite shoulder, "Support it with your good hand." He picked up her handbag which lay half open. Kitty fought the panic that he might realise her cigarette lighter hid a secret camera, but he was too invested in her injury to pay any attention to her bag, which he placed over her good arm.

Kitty was surprised at his manners, she imagined all Germans to be curt, rude, and difficult. This was the first evidence that they were also human, and she wasn't sure how it made her feel. He placed his arm around her waist and slowly guided her towards the hospital. Her heart thumped, as she grew near to the place she desperately needed to get inside, and hoped the pain she was experiencing was worth any information she could gather.

He pushed through the large double doors and ushered her inside towards an antique walnut desk, where a French medic sat. The odour of disinfectant tickled her nose and she marvelled at the sparklingly clean interior.

"This lady has fallen over and, by the looks of it, broken two fingers, I would like her to be seen."

"This facility is for German military personnel only." The medic refused to look up and continued to work on an extensive list of names. Kitty was surprised that a French citizen would be working there and refuse to allow treatment.

"And I am asking that you make an exception. She is in a lot of pain and her fingers are swelling by the second, which is not a good sign." The German puffed out his chest and his face flushed.

The man, sat behind the desk, stood up and pointed to the door. "I have orders, and I cannot permit you any further. Now please, take her somewhere else."

KITTY TAYLOR by Sarah Colliver

Frederick's face flushed, and he leaned in close to the man. "Get the most senior officer down here now, or it's ME you will need to worry about." He slammed his fist on the desk.

There it was, the aggressor side, the invader. How quickly the niceties could evaporate and morph into threats and anger. She whimpered and wobbled, to increase his concern.

Frederick guided her to a wooden chair, next to a small table with a jug of water. "Please sit here whilst I sort this out. Here, take a sip," he said gently as he poured a half glass. "You look so pale."

Kitty was grateful for the water; her mouth was claggy. She slowly sipped and watched the scene unfold.

A uniformed man burst through a door behind the desk, with a chest full of medals and fury on his face, but it was soon replaced with warm recognition as he embraced her rescuer. They exchanged loud pleasantries in German, before turning towards Kitty. She suddenly felt exposed, having no clue what was being said, an inner dialogue of 'what ifs' began to roll.

KITTY TAYLOR by Sarah Colliver

She had put herself in more danger than she could have realised.

"Please, come with me. What is your name?"

"Giselle Lavigne."

"Pleased to meet you, Madamoiselle Lavigne. We are going to make you more comfortable and perhaps put a splint on your fingers."

The thought of disappearing from sight, with two officers of the Reich, made the hair on the back of her neck stand. This could be the end of her, she was utterly defenceless against them, whatever they wanted to do. But she had no choice. If she ran, she was dead, because why would she run for no reason?

She stood slowly. "Thank you, Frederick. You are so kind."

"Shall I stay with you? Hans doesn't speak much French. My Grandmother was from Normandy, that's why my French is so good-it is, don't you think?"

Kitty fought a gasp; he didn't look much older than her. He too had a French grandparent, like her. Maybe he, like her, would have done anything to get back to

KITTY TAYLOR by Sarah Colliver

France, war, or no war. She began to soften towards him. Perhaps they weren't so dissimilar? And then she remembered that he was part of an aggressive force which had brutalised their way through her beloved France, and that was totally the opposite of why she was there. She snapped back into the moment and remembered the job she had to. There was no room for emotion, that only complicated things.

Valerie's concerned face peered out from her kitchen window. How long she had watched the street, Kitty did not know, but hours she suspected. Kitty waved and pointed to her freshly bandaged hand and before she could reach the shop, Valerie flung open the door and swept her up into a tight embrace. "Cherie, I was so worried. Come in, come in." She ushered her inside the shop door and locked up again behind them. "What's happened? Are you okay? You've been gone so long! I didn't know what happened..."

"Aunty, I'm fine! It's only a little injury, but I'm not sure how much use I'll be in here, although I can still serve and tidy."

"Up! Up!" Valerie steered her up the stairs. "I want to get a look at you. Oh, I've been a mess."

KITTY TAYLOR by Sarah Colliver

"I fell, that's all. And kind officer of the Reich escorted me into an 'extremely German' hospital to be treated. Somewhat of a ladies man, and I fear I may have led him on a little..." Kitty stopped and realised she must consider what else she said. "It's just, I couldn't risk being rude to him, so I had to be appreciative, you know?"

"Yes, they have enormous egos, and don't like to feel undermined. What else could you do?" Valerie lit them both a cigarette and handed Kitty one. "Sit here, you must be exhausted."

Kitty always knew when she needed to rest, because her clear mind became clouded, it became difficult to manage what she should and shouldn't say. "I'll have this, and then lay down, if you don't mind. Looks like you could do with having a rest too. Have you been this tense the whole time?"

"Yes. I agree. A nap would be useful for us both."

Kitty loved living with Valerie, but the concern for Kitty was taking a toll, and she may need to think about moving on to a new place. If Valerie became too nervous, she could slip up, and they would all be at risk.

KITTY TAYLOR by Sarah Colliver

Besides that, (the official reason), Kitty cared for her and couldn't bear to see her face taut with fear.

Kitty kissed her cheek and stubbed out the cigarette. "Merci." She headed into her room and closed the door behind her with a heavy sigh. She rubbed her forehead - her brain swirled with information. Tomorrow she would get a message to Florin to send to London. The 'hospital' was a fair target, not being open for treating anyone other than Germans. Although inside for a relatively brief time, her gift for noticing stored every detail she could. The lack of patients, the heavily guarded area at the back, the many restricted rooms. There was more to the place than they implied on the outside.

Sebastian, Henri, Frederick, Valerie, Raymond, Lucile. People all caught up in the death, murder and destruction of war. She slumped onto her bed and without even taking off her shoes, curled up and instantly fell into a deep, much needed, sleep.

Sudden banging on the shop door yanked her from her restorative slumber. She jumped out of bed, startled, hopping around and unsure what was happening. Was it the Gestapo? Would they bang on the door first or simply kick it in? Her fingers throbbed and she winced in pain as she fought to slow her breathing.

"It's okay Cherie, it's angry customers, they're hungry!" Valerie called up the stairs. Kitty caught her reflection in the full-length mirror, and realised she was still fully clothed including her shoes.

"We have nothing! There is NOTHING!" Valerie called to the queuing shoppers.

Kitty headed downstairs towards her, curious as to what was going on, and relieved there was no arresting party pointing guns at them. "Why is the shop empty? What will we do?"

"Nothing to bake with, supplier was arrested yesterday, and so we have nothing to bake. They sound like they're going to break the door down."

"Tell them to come back after two."

"Huh?" Valerie scratched her head. "What would be the point?"

"Well, for now, it will stop them banging the door, but also I may have an idea."

KITTY TAYLOR by Sarah Colliver

"Okay. Worth a try." Valerie grabbed a pencil, a scrap of paper, and scribbled a note which she folded in half so that it stood in the window. "Come back at 2pm."

A murmuring crowd headed off towards the fish shop, as Kitty shuffled to the bathroom for a wash and to clean her teeth. Her brain was clear and felt refreshed from her sleep. Valerie followed behind like a child hoping for a treat.

"You feeling better? You look better."

"Best night's sleep I've had since being here, in spite of this." She waved her bandaged hand. "Much needed. Let me brush my teeth, how about some coffee?"

"Oui, good idea. Come down when you are ready."

Kitty washed up and changed her clothes. Her stomach grumbled, begging for food. She must have slept for hours.

"Here, Cherie. Hungry? I have a little bread. How's your hand?" Valerie's voice was full of concern.

Kitty sat down at the table which, unusually, was covered in crumbs. An indication of the state Valerie had been in. As if she could read Kitty's thoughts, she began to wipe the crumbs into a pile and onto her open cupped hand, with a little nod.

"It's okay. I'm fine. Anyway, my idea - I thought that if we cannot get anything to make the bread, how about getting hold of onions and garlic, we could make soup- I have a recipe I used to make in Lon…" Kitty paused, "a recipe which my grand-mère taught me. It might help stave off hunger and stop them beating down our door! What happened to your supplier? Why was he arrested?" Kitty hoped he knew nothing about her and wouldn't lead anyone to them.

"He was caught hiding two Jewish children. I say caught; someone must have informed on him. I don't understand why anyone would do that. What the hell is wrong with the world? Those poor little things, they have done nothing wrong, committed no crime, they're innocents. What kind of grown man could feel so threatened by a child, that they need to imprison and murder them?" Valerie spoke quickly and then her voice trailed into sobs. "Starving little people, forced to hide away in cellars and behind walls, like dirty secrets, not allowed to make a sound even. And why? Because of their religion?"

KITTY TAYLOR by Sarah Colliver

Kitty stood and hugged Valerie tightly, rubbing her back in rhythmic circles. "I wish I could make sense of it all, but I have no words. We can only keep doing what we can, in our own ways, and hope that eventually those evil pigs will be beaten."

Valerie pulled back and leant against the wall. She fiddled with her plant, but Kitty knew this was her way of pulling herself together.

Kitty spoke softly, "I constantly move things out of my mind. Anything which threatens my ability to do my job, to blend in here, to survive. It's a battle I face moment to moment, like a washerwoman sorting washing into piles. I know I have so much stored up in there, dark things which I have pushed away. One day they will be back, I only hope I'll have the energy and capacity to deal with them. Until then, we do what we can, non?"

Valerie smiled and nodded. "So wise and yet so young." She sniffed and stood up straight. "Yes, we must remind ourselves not everyone in the world is bad. Look at you, here to help us. And the grocer who tried to save the children. Even the officer who took you for treatment at the hospital, he wasn't all bad was he?"

KITTY TAYLOR by Sarah Colliver

Kitty shifted her weight, "He was probably after 'gratitude' from me, they don't do anything without an ulterior motive." Deep down, she thought back to how he asked her for nothing in return. How he spoke of his grandparents, how he insisted she get treatment. None of that was bad, or nasty...

Valerie chewed her cheek and fiddled with the tablecloth. She was on edge, not surprising considering she was harbouring an enemy of Germany, punishable by death. She sighed and touched Kitty's cheek. "Now Cherie, one of my, 'friends' can get me the onions..." Valerie grabbed her handbag from the hook and slipped on her jacket. She checked her reflection in the mirror tidied her hair. "I know where he will be right now, I won't be long." She kissed Kitty's cheeks and, in a blur, was gone.

Kitty smiled and reached up onto the shelf for the old tin with the cow on. Thank goodness there was a cigarette. Alone, and in peace, she digested the information, managing to sort it out and into order. She would get a message to Florin via Lucile, to make sure he sent everything she knew to London. That was first. Sebastian, what to do about him? They were in the same town, for the same reason, and this meant their worlds were going to collide. She needed a strategy to keep them safe whilst navigating their situation. Why was he there, and how long had he been there? She needed to meet with him. She would leave him a message, but it needed to be in a way that looked like a letter between friends. Perhaps Valerie had writing paper, or an old postcard she could use.

Kitty's eyes streamed as Valerie chopped the mountain of onions. "He must like you a lot to give you this many!"

"He asked me to marry him once, but, you know, I don't want to give this all up- become a slave to a man again. This way I can be adored, and showered with onions, but keep my independence." Valerie laughed, "Once upon a time it would be perfume or flowers, now it's onions and I couldn't be more thankful!"

"I feel the same, I don't want to be tied to a man. I have things I want to do; a man would make it all about him and his needs. One day I am going to move back to France and start up my own café or boulangerie. I have been saving for a long time."

KITTY TAYLOR by Sarah Colliver

"Is that why you came, Cherie?"

"I longed to be back, yes. But I needed to help if I could…" Kitty was aware they were crossing the line. "My recipe is authentic and so popular that where I used to work, people came in solely for this. It will be interesting to see how it fares over here!"

"Well, if it saves our door from being bashed in, until we can get hold of what we need for the bread, then I am up for it…I trust you, and cannot wait to try it. Oh, I left paper and envelopes on the table for you, with my fountain pen and ink too. Much more acceptable than a pencil, don't you think?" Valerie winked and smiled.

"Thank you. I will help you to finish this, and perhaps once the rush dies down, I can nip out and deliver it."

By 1.30pm, a queue had already formed outside the boulangerie, alive with curious chattering about what they would be offered. The delicious waft from the final minutes of the soup cooking, increased the noise from the crowd as they longed to fill their bellies. Valerie opened the window to address the queue, "Please come back with a vessel to transport your soup. We cannot offer any bread today, but I can assure you that

KITTY TAYLOR by Sarah Colliver

the onion soup which my niece has created, from a traditional family recipe, is going to be worth the effort from you. But you will need a container for us to serve it to you in, to take home. So please, come back when you have this, and at 2pm I will open the door."

The hungry queue dissolved temporarily, and Valerie squealed with delight. "Cherie, maybe we could do this weekly? If it goes well today? I'm sure my friend can continue to supply us with the onions."

Kitty beamed. Valerie appeared ten years younger when she smiled, and the anxiety was lifted for a while. It felt nice to have brought her joy, instead of threats of arrest and torture. She shrugged the thoughts away and tested the soup, which seemed even tastier than when she last made it, so far away, back home.

Kitty hoped she didn't reek of onion and garlic, as she meandered through the quieter streets, beneath the late afternoon sun. She deliberately took the long way, to avoid the square where she had witnessed the brutal murder. Pausing along the way on numerous benches, or to gaze into a shop window, she remained vigilant, checking constantly for anyone who may be watching her. Before leaving, as she wrote the note,

KITTY TAYLOR by Sarah Colliver

she struggled to recall the name Sebastian had told her, but knew it began with an M, so decided to use the first letters of his name, like a mysterious love note to anyone who happened across it.

She arrived at the square with the fountain, across from his green door, and hung back, pausing for a moment. A clock on a nearby church chimed and a scrawny black cat licked himself under the shade of a bench. The window was closed, and an image of Sebastian stood naked, when she last saw him, flashed through her mind, and stirred something inside. What was it about him that had such power over her? She inched slowly towards his house, poised to put the letter through the door, and scurry away without drawing attention. Inviting him to meet her away from prying eyes. But nothing is ever that easy or simple, and before she could post the letter, the shabby green door opened, and there stood Sebastian.

He pulled her inside by the front of her jacket and closed the door. "Have you been cooking onions?"

Kitty couldn't help but laugh, "Funnily enough, yes."

KITTY TAYLOR by Sarah Colliver

"What's with the bandage, you ok?" Sebastian seemed genuinely concerned.

"This? It's nothing. I took a tumble, and these bore the brunt. Painful but I'll live."

"Good. So, coffee? Well in a loose way, it isn't anything like real coffee, is it?" He was already up the stairs heading to his kitchen area.

Kitty followed him and relaxed a little. They were at least off the street and not visible to any watchers, and she was quite sure no one had spotted her arrival. "Sure."

"I knew you'd be back. Just a matter of time. We're good together, you and me. It's not like that with anyone else."

Kitty prickled at the thought of him with other women. It hadn't occurred to her before. Her face flushed and her nostrils flared a little. "I'm not here for *that*. And believe it or not you aren't completely irresistible, despite what you think."

Sebastian whipped around to face her, their close proximity in his small kitchen area made it impossible for her to step away. He stared into her eyes, with an intensity which reached inside and sped up her heart. Neither looked away, caught in a strange moment fused with anger, frustration, and confusion.

"You don't want me anymore?" he whispered and gently rubbed the tip of his nose along her cheek and forehead. She stifled a moan as her rationale disintegrated and her burning desire returned. "I think about you all the time-about holding you, touching you, kissing you." He pressed his lips to hers for a second. "To know you are here and to not be able to have you- its torture. I can't think, I can't sleep, because when I close my eyes, I see you, Kitty."

She jolted back into the moment. "Don't call me that." She wriggled out of his tight embrace and out onto the landing. "Almost had me again. Is this what you do, is this your seduction routine? When you want something, you pretend to care?"

Sebastian turned back to the half-made coffee and finished making them. "Here." He handed her a cup of steaming black liquid and headed out to the small room at the back, which was set up as a lounge, with two armchairs and a standard lamp. He slumped deep into one of the chairs and spread his legs, which meant when Kitty sat, she had no choice but to touch his knee with her own.

"Why are you here, in Fornay?" Her direct question startled him, but he tried hard to hide it.

"I came from Lyon. When our circuit was infiltrated, the rest of us dispersed. I was told to lay low for a while, try and make contact with people here, to see what support I could offer, and then possibly return to England. They have concerns that my face is becoming too known in France now. This isn't my first trip, if you know what I mean."

"Right. So, what do you need?"

"New orders. Or a plane home. I've been here three weeks now and heard nothing. Only contact I knew of was Henri, and he's dead, I presume. Luckily, that's how I found you; or I'd still be on my own. I was watching him, wondering if it would be safe to make contact. But it was too late to help him." Sebastian shook his head and swore under his breath.

"We must keep this separate. What we had, Kitty and Sebastian, we can't do that here. It isn't safe. There's too much at stake." Kitty meant it, but she also had to acknowledge that his implication of other women was a turn off for her, and made him less appealing the more she considered that perhaps he was just a womaniser. An expert one at that, but nevertheless not anything she was interested in pursuing. "How did you find this place, to stay?"

"I had the sense to get a contact to make me an extra set of new identity papers, under the name of 'Michel Bernard,' which I kept hidden. I knew if things blew up, it would ensure I could leave under a different name. I saw this place was advertised for rent, and so, I'm here," he shrugged. "But I only have this place for another week."

"How are you for money, and what's your cover story for being here, if you get stopped?"

"Workplace injury- to my vision. I'm here to recover. I don't plan to get stopped; I only go as far as the nearest shop. Except when I was watching Henri. I used all my cash up paying the rent for this, which she insisted on having in advance. On my last few centimes now."

KITTY TAYLOR by Sarah Colliver

"Okay." Kitty opened her handbag and carefully reached inside the lining, where money was hidden. "Here, this should tide you over, help you buy food at least."

"Help me get out of here, soon. I'm going crazy waiting." His eyes darkened.

"Leave it with me and I will see what we can do. I'm not risking coming back here again, so will leave you a message." Kitty racked her brains for a safe place to hide a note. "On the outskirts of town, there's a ruin of an old bakery. Where the remains of the bread ovens are, I will leave you a message. I don't need to tell you the importance of being extra careful right now. It's feeling like everything is closing in a bit."

Sebastian took her hand and kissed it. "I know you think that I'm saying things to get you into bed, and if I am you can't blame me…we go together like wine and cheese…"

"Wine and cheese?" Kitty's face crumpled with disgust.

"Okay, don't judge me, I'm hungry and frisky…" He shrugged his shoulders and then laughed. "Seriously though, there hasn't ever been anyone like you. And seeing you like this, so capable and in control, well, to me you are more appealing than ever." He kissed her hand again and placed it back on her knee.

Kitty stood up, unsure what to believe, but feeling powerful that this would be the first time they parted without going to bed. And that was solely down to her. She stood tall and smiled inwardly. "Remember how many lives count on us being careful. Don't see me out, I will slip away quietly. In fact, do you have a back door?"

Sebastian looked taken aback, but only for a millisecond. "Yes, if I can find the key. Hold on." He headed downstairs and she could hear him fumbling around, with cupboard doors banging and drawers rifled. She headed down after him, to see what the noise was.

"What are you doing?" Kitty scratched her head. "It's no big deal. If you don't use the back, it may be safer not to draw attention by using it anyway."

"Yes, you're right." He rubbed her arm.

"Although, find that key, because one day you may need an alternative escape route, and we have to think about every eventuality."

"I think I'm field-fatigued. Not thinking as clearly as I could be." He shook his head and muttered under his breath.

"Leave this with me. I think it's time to get you home." Kitty slipped quietly away, keeping to the shadows until she turned the corner onto the next street. She mulled over his demeanour and decided to ask London to send a plane to get him out of France. She would head to the barn and see if there was word from London about the hospital information she had sent too.

ASSISTANCE REQUIRED

Lucile and Raymond were already at the barn, and Kitty was beginning to wonder if it had become their love- nest. Raymond was married to a much older woman who seemed to 'turn a blind eye' to his strange comings and goings. She wasn't a resistance member herself but would never betray her young and virile man.

KITTY TAYLOR by Sarah Colliver

"That colour suits you, Raymond." Kitty pointed towards him.

"Huh?" He looked down at his beige stripey shirt and black trousers.

"The lipstick, I mean." She smiled and turned away as Lucile frantically rubbed at his face with her neck scarf. "Look, whatever you two get up to is none of my business. You'll get no judgment from me, as long as it doesn't affect your security. Now, sit and update me. What have London said?"

"Okay. Well, they are happy with your report about the so-called hospital and have given the go ahead to destroy it. They don't need the photographs after all, which is a good job - as my contact has been unable to take any yet, too risky. London wanted it done from the ground initially but decided to locate the target from above and bomb it, which will also avoid retaliation on the locals. Last time there was an action carried out by the resistance, the Germans shot 100 from the surrounding villages."

Kitty's conflicting emotions bubbled in her stomach. She had played a part in fighting back, but the trouble was, she would now have the lives of innocent civilians, inevitably caught up in the bombing raid on her conscience. Either way, people would die. At least this way there would be no executions. "Can you get another message to them? I have made contact with someone from the Lyon circuit, and he needs to be lifted out, as soon as possible. The name he is under is Michel Bernard. No, that's not going to work…" Kitty remembered he was using the extra set of papers he'd had locally made. London would not identify him by that name. "Sebastian Fabre. I don't have his codename. But London should figure it out. When you hear back, let me know and I will tell you where to leave the message for him Lucile."

"Okay. Leave it with me." Lucile brushed a quick kiss over Raymond's cheek and squeezed his hand. "À bientôt."

He watched her leave before turning to Kitty. "I love her, everything about her."

"It's not my business. The less I know the better. It does complicate things though. The deeper the feelings, the more they can be used against you, in times of…"

"I'm not stupid. But what can you do? You can't help who you love. Even in war, there is love."

Kitty sighed. She couldn't take this on too. "Henri? What have you heard?"

"Not good. They got as much information as beating a man to a pulp can release. But it was all outdated, and nothing they didn't already know. Once they were finished, they took him out and shot him. It would have been a relief for him in the end. Bastards."

Kitty shook her head, her face red with anger. "What chance do we have, any of us, when we don't know who the next informant will be?"

"We must trust that what we are doing will make a difference. And like you always tell us Giselle, we must be extra careful. We cannot do any more than that." Raymond's eyes filled with compassion and concern.

"It's not enough though. Is it?" Kitty stood and chewed her fingernail.

"Here." Raymond offered her a cigarette. "Looks like you could do with one."

KITTY TAYLOR by Sarah Colliver

He threw her a box of matches which she caught awkwardly with her injured hand. "Ouch!" she winced and stood still for a moment waiting for the pain to subside.

"Here, let me." Raymond took back the matches, and struck one, placing it on the end of her cigarette. "I know we haven't always exactly got on well, but, Giselle, you have guts, and I respect you for that."

Kitty smiled and felt suddenly weary. She slumped onto a hay bale and took the moment to enjoy her cigarette. They sat in comfortable silence awaiting Lucile's return.

As Kitty rounded the corner to home, Madame Thomas watched her arrival as she surveyed the street from her rickety stool beneath her window. With her cat ready to pounce beside her, Kitty thought she looked witchy. "How's your hand, dear Giselle? Not much use to poor Valerie like that are you? Broken, is it?"

"Oh, it'll be right soon enough. Thank you for your concern though, I am most touched." Kitty spoke but continued walking until she reached the door of the boulangerie. "Good day, Madame." How much did she know or suspect, she wondered. It was a worry, but not one she had control over. Valerie and she behaved exactly like kin, and she was confident there was nothing odd to cause suspicion in that way. Unless she was a keen observer at night and caught sight of Kitty returning after curfew.

Valerie was not home, so Kitty busied herself putting away the measly provisions she had managed to buy for them to eat. It was proving more difficult every day to source what they needed for the shop, and they seemed to make less and less bread. The onions were not as forthcoming as they initially hoped, and Kitty suspected that Valerie's 'friend' was a black marketeer, which made their situation dicey. They couldn't afford to draw attention to themselves. Perhaps she should talk to her, discuss closing for a couple of weeks, make it known that they aren't able to get hold of any 'extras.' It would almost be time for her to leave then, she suspected. She was only supposed to be out there for six weeks, and she was in her seventh already.

Kitty checked the soil in the potted plants; they needed a water. It was unlike Valerie to forget. Kitty filled a large glass jug with water and, one by one, drenched their parched soil. She imagined them crying out with appreciation and smiled. "You're welcome!" she answered.

It would be strange to be back home, to adapt to the changes. Getting used to the air raids again, would take time, as since she had been in France there had only been one locally. Here it wasn't the skies where fear came from; the enemy wandered past in the street or sat behind them in the cafés. They were actual people rather than aeroplanes in the sky. Still, she would have to make it through the next few days to make it home, and, in her current situation, a lot could happen in that time. Life, death, and anything in between.

"Cherie?" Valerie called from the shop; Kitty could hear her locking the door followed by footsteps on the stairs.

"Oui, here in the lounge! I'm giving your thirsty plants a water!"

"Ahh, I knew I meant to do something before I left. Merci Cherie. What would I do without you?"

Kitty said nothing about the fact that she would soon be gone, she had no concrete information anyway. She would tell her only when she was leaving. She would tell Valerie to moan loudly about her disgust for her niece, leaving in the middle of the night with a man. The more she would moan, the less suspicion.

"I think we should shut the shop for a while, let it be known that we cannot get hold of anything. They are really cracking down on the black market right now. We don't want to lead anyone to our door. Are you sure your 'friend' is safe?"

Valerie stared at Kitty, her mouth gaping, her hands on her hips. "I told you, of course he is safe. He would never put me in any danger." Her voice raised to not quite a shout, but louder than usual. "You really mean it, we should shut the shop, just like that?" Her cheeks flushed. "So now, not only do I have the Germans dictating to me how to live, but also the British?"

Kitty gasped, "What is it? This isn't like you."

Valerie turned away and stared out of the back window, over the courtyard. "We must get out there and tidy up, it's a mess."

"What's happened?" Concern rose to the back of Kitty's throat.

KITTY TAYLOR by Sarah Colliver

"I'm so very sick of it all," Valerie's defeated voice was almost a whisper.

"It's me, I'm causing you too much stress, being here…"

"Don't say that. You have become family to me. It's not you. You help me manage the insanity." Valerie stared with sad eyes at Kitty.

Insanity was the correct definition for everything going on. Something was wrong. It was time for Kitty to leave. Hopefully, it would be set for the next few days.

"Sit down, Aunty." Kitty pulled out a chair. "Take a moment and think. We could come up with ideas to bring in money."

"It's not about money. I'm well provided for should I need it. I…I've had enough, that's all. Enough of rubbing shoulders with people who would sooner report you to the Gestapo than help you. Smiling politely when I want to scream. Scrounging cigarettes because we, mere women, are no longer permitted any. Watching people dragged off the streets for the smallest of wrongdoing, no, for doing NOTHING! Sick of knowing how many people are dying every day, whilst we navigate this confusing state of new normality." Valerie

KITTY TAYLOR by Sarah Colliver

shuddered and then sobbed. Deep, racking, body jolting sobs. Her hands shook, and her mouth quivered.

Kitty crouched next to her and whispered, "All of this, it's all true, it is enough to drive us all mad."

Valerie wrung her hands. "There is something else...I came across town a few nights ago, right before curfew. Same route I always take back from my 'friend's' house. Two drunk soldiers staggered out of the Trumpet bar and knocked into me."

Kitty's hand flew to her mouth, she hoped she was wrong about what she was about to be told.

"They pushed me down a dark alleyway and...he ripped my skirt, and the other one had his hands around my neck." She untied her silk scarf and placed it on the table. Red marks and black bruising circled her neck.

"Oh! No, no, no!"

"No, no, Giselle. Not that. Lucky for me they were so drunk and unsteady on their feet. I fought my way out of their grip and ran home. I didn't want to say anything, you have enough to deal with." She clenched Kitty's hand. "It's knocked me, my confidence, that's all. I was the lucky one, I know plenty who haven't been as lucky. Often, they are found dead in the river once they've had their 'fun' with them."

Kitty stood and sighed. "I don't know what to say. No wonder you are feeling so overwhelmed. Perhaps you too should lay low for a while, recover. Shutting the shop may be a blessing. I'm only suggesting it to try and keep you safe. Fat chance of that, after what you've told me. Not safe anywhere here."

"It's fine. I'm okay and feel better for telling you. And you're right, I will put a notice up in the window. Let's say we close for two weeks, eh? We can spread the word that we have had another family bereavement and need time to get things organised?"

"No, let's keep as close to the truth as possible. We close because we have nothing to sell now. It is easier than creating a whole scenario."

Valerie nodded, "Oui. And for me, it can be a welcome break, away from prying people every day who don't come in for food, but to spy, I am sure of it... Perhaps I can even tackle the courtyard, tidy it up. It's a disgrace now. When my husband was alive, he kept it lovely. We even grew flowers and would sit and enjoy our coffee together in the morning."

"I will help you- it might be a good distraction for us both!"

Valerie stood and threw her arms around Kitty. "I would love that."

"Bon, now I must go. But I will see you later." Kitty kissed Valerie on both cheeks and headed downstairs and out through the shop.

It took twice as long to get anywhere with her broken fingers, as they were still too painful to ride her bicycle. The barn felt like forever away, whereas she could ride there in 15 minutes. She dare not run anywhere, as it drew attention, and people assumed you had something to hide. Shame because she was a steady and competent runner. She decided to make the most of her stroll, with the sun on her face and the gentle breeze. All appeared calm in town, and she absorbed the wonderful feeling of uneventfulness.

With the town behind her she took the steep shortcut, only manageable on foot through the shady trees, stopping briefly to observe a small deer who had frozen with her arrival. For a moment they stared at each other before it darted away to safety. Kitty hoped Lucile would have news of the next plane. Valerie's nerves were fraying, and their neighbour was becoming increasingly observant. It would only be a matter of time before it was no longer a safe-haven.

Raymond stood outside the barn, smoking a cigarette, his face to the sun. He looked tired. "Bonjour, ça va?"

Raymond opened his eyes and turned to Kitty, "Giselle, Lucile is inside. I will be in soon."

"Is everything ok?" Kitty wondered if the love birds had fought.

"It hasn't been ok for a long time, you know that." He spat on the floor.

Kitty headed past him into the barn. Lucile was laying on the straw, she half smiled.

"What's up? What's going on?"

"Don't ask." Lucile picked a piece of hay apart and sprinkled it onto the floor.

KITTY TAYLOR by Sarah Colliver

"I'm asking, what the hell is going on? Is it London, Florin?" Kitty felt panic arise in the pit of her stomach.

"No, no. Florin is still safe, and I have information on the scheduled pick up…"

Kitty and Lucile froze. Grunts from a scuffle outside meant they both slowly reached for their pistols and edged towards the door in silence. Raymond was on the floor punching a person beneath him.

"Stop!" Kitty shouted and pointed her pistol towards the tangle of arms and legs.

Raymond eased away from the intruder and stepped backwards.

Kitty gasped, "How did you find us?"

"I followed you," Sebastian said.

"So much for being extra careful," Raymond cursed and pulled Sebastian up by the scruff of his neck, pushing him inside. "It seems you know this man, Giselle?"

Kitty and Lucile followed, closing the door behind them. "Sit." Raymond pointed to a hay bale and roughly pushed Sebastian onto it. "You should know better than to sneak up somewhere you aren't expected."

Kitty's anger rose and she felt like she might explode. Finally earning the respect of Raymond, only for it to be blown apart by Sebastian. She struggled to find the right words to say.

"Well Lucile, this is Michel, or should I say Sebastian, the one you have been trying to arrange to get home. Looks like that is the right call, since he is behaving so recklessly."

"I had nowhere to go. My landlady evicted me, I thought this was a safer option than being picked up off the street, or loitering. Doesn't take much for people to be suspicious. Would you rather I knock on the boulangerie and ask Valerie to put me up for a bit."

"How long have you been tailing me?" Kitty's words escaped with venom.

"Not long. I thought this was the safest option, away from all the twitching curtains."

Raymond stared at Kitty. She thought he was about to chastise her again, but he said nothing. How could she have been so unaware, where was her sixth sense? The truth was, a sixth sense was not enough in the field, you needed double that to cope with the layers of deceit.

"Maybe this was the better option. He is here now, he stays, until he is lifted out. He can lay low, and sleep tucked up there." Lucile pointed to the hayloft.

Kitty nodded but could not look at Sebastian. He had made her appear stupid and incompetent.

"Lucile, a word?" Kitty headed out of the barn, closely followed by Lucile. "You were saying, about the orders from London?"

"They are going to do the lift out, the same night as the bombing of the hospital. You and Sebastian are to leave and two new arrivals will be brought. It will be tomorrow night, weather dependent. For the final go ahead, we need to listen out for the following message tomorrow morning on the radio. 'The pale girl has gone to heaven.'"

"Okay. One other thing: don't give any information to Sebastian. He is incapable of making good choices right now, so let's keep him in the dark. Oui?"

KITTY TAYLOR by Sarah Colliver

Lucile nodded. "I understand. He seems like a loose cannon, to be honest."

"Hmm, it does feel that way. Anyway, what about you? What's going on?"

"You really want to know? Because you're not going to like it, not one bit."

Kitty studied Lucile's paled face, she looked exhausted. "You're pregnant, aren't you?"

Lucile nodded and stared at the ground.

"Shit." Kitty shook her head. "You need to leave, get home. You can't have a baby here."

"I'm not leaving. I can't leave him."

"But he's married," Kitty spoke in a low voice.

"Yes, we are aware of that," Lucile sighed. "Stop judging me, I know what they call babies who are born outside of marriage. You don't need to remind me of that."

"Hey! Don't accuse me of that. I never said a word." Kitty reflected on her own family history for a second.

KITTY TAYLOR by Sarah Colliver

"You know this is messy, and not possible Lucile, you cannot have a baby like this. I order you to leave on that plane. You will take my place." Kitty's heart pounded.

"You cannot force me to leave. I bet London would rather I stay and carry on. Besides Raymond has a plan, when the baby is born, he will take it to his wife and say he found it abandoned. She never had children. She will look after it. I will carry on working. At the end of the war, who knows?"

"So, you have your own plan then? And you are going to disobey orders?"

Lucile nodded. "Please don't tell them, I will get a message through once you are home. I won't be able to hide it from Florin forever anyway, and he has direct contact. I want you back safe first."

Kitty sighed. The complexities were becoming too much, and she felt drained. "Okay. They won't hear it from me." Then she thought of the many times she and Sebastian had enjoyed; she had been lucky not to fall herself. What irony that would have been, after everything she felt towards her mother.

KITTY TAYLOR by Sarah Colliver

They headed back into the barn where Raymond was pouring wine for each of them.

"Until the drop, which will also lift you out of here, you lie low. I mean it, you do not leave, you speak to no one, and you do as you're told. Coming here was stupid, and you endangered us all." Kitty didn't even try and hide the anger she felt.

"Not sure who put you in charge, but it suits you. I understand." Sebastian winked.

"A word, outside." She gestured for him to follow her, and he slumped arrogantly against the ivy which crept up the outside of the stone barn wall.

"Well?" he asked.

"Stop it. I don't want them to know anything, they do not need to know that anything has passed between us. Please do this for me. You have already made me look like a fool, please don't make me look like a whore too."

Sebastian smiled. "Understood. My lips are sealed. I promise."

KITTY TAYLOR by Sarah Colliver

Kitty should have felt relieved, but she didn't. Something about him was off. And she no longer trusted his word. He should not have followed her to the barn. He could have approached her alone on the way in the woods. He knew what he was doing. She would alert Raymond to watch him and advise them to stay at the barn too. Tonight would be her last night with Valerie. She would head to the barn early morning; it was safer out of town, out of sight, for the final few hours.

KITTY TAYLOR by Sarah Colliver

WHICH WAY TO TURN?

Kitty lay awake, listening to the rhythmic ticking of the clock. Her mind pondering the most recent events. Any desire she once had for Sebastian had evaporated, and she felt betrayed and belittled by his actions. He was more experienced than her, shouldn't he know better? He told her this wasn't his first visit, so why put her in that position? Maybe he felt threatened by her capabilities. He certainly liked to think of her bound to the kitchen or the bedroom. A chill crept across her body as a new dark thought popped into her already busy mind. Sebastian crossed her path as Henri was being arrested, he said he had been 'lying low' for three weeks and seemed to be an expert in tailing people without being noticed. She was usually excellent at noticing things and had not suspected a thing. Perhaps he had been following Philippe when she first arrived? Maybe he was a double-agent. London had not warned them, so they too were in the dark. Thank goodness she told Raymond to watch him. At least he was alerted to her hunch that all may not be as it seemed. Her flesh crawled with the memory of him sweet talking her into bed all those times, and how he must have laughed at her naivety.

KITTY TAYLOR by Sarah Colliver

Tomorrow she would leave Valerie, and by Tuesday, might even be back in London. She would be sad to leave her. They had grown close, but she felt relieved that Valerie would still have her 'friend' for company; Kitty wasn't leaving her alone. It was impossible not to form attachments living under the same roof, even though all through training you were warned against this. It made you drop your guard, say a little too much, relax. All those things could only end in capture, torture, unthinkable thoughts. She squeezed her eyes shut and pushed the images away. Isn't that what Sebastian had done – caused her to immediately drop her guard, when she jumped into bed with him? He clouded her mind and muddied the already murky water.

What if he really was a double agent, should he still fly back? Would they then deal with him? What evidence did she have anyway, other than a hunch that things weren't quite right? She could ask London what they thought she should do, but that could add days onto the scheduled pickup and maybe jeopardise the whole circuit. Should she warn Valerie about the impending air raid? She knew the answer, and took comfort in the knowledge that the boulangerie was on the opposite side of town. Surely, they would be accurate enough to bomb only the target and not the civilian population.

She had already gathered her belongings, reaching behind the nook next to the window, where she had hidden her revolver. She would take only what she had brought with her and leave no traces behind. She could disappear like a phantom.

At six, she washed and dressed, and headed downstairs with her bag, which she hung on the hook on the back of the understairs cupboard. She took a last wander around the empty, quiet shop, peeking up the street from the window. No signs of life, and what looked like the beginnings of a beautiful sunny day. A movement caught her eye; it was Madame Thomas with her finger to her lips, and the other hand beckoning her over. Kitty, immediately alarmed, wondered what to do, was this a trap? If she ignored her, it looked bad. No, she should feign ignorance and investigate. She tiptoed out of the shop, and across the silent street.

"In here," she whispered, pushing Kitty in through her door. Her house was cosy but basic. Clean and functional.

KITTY TAYLOR by Sarah Colliver

"Madame? Are you ok? Do you need my help?" Kitty asked in her most innocent voice.

"Just listen to me. I don't know who you are. But you are in danger."

Kitty wobbled.

"Your 'aunty,' Madame Aubert, you know she was attacked the other night?"

"Oh that! Yes, she told me all about it. She has been quite shaken you know…"

"Shh girl, let me finish. I don't think she has told you the whole story, because her 'friend' saved her from them."

"No, she didn't mention that, but thank goodness he was around, it makes me shiver to think what may have happened if he hadn't…"

"Do you always talk this much when somebody is trying to help you?"

Kitty shook her head, and her face twisted in confusion.

"Her 'friend' is a German officer."

KITTY TAYLOR by Sarah Colliver

Kitty's hand flew to her gaping mouth. That was why Valerie was so stressed lately. Why she wanted to keep her 'friend' such a secret.

"So, you see, you must leave soon. What if he were to pay her an unexpected visit? Word is getting around now too, and it won't be long before no one visits her shop...because of what she is – a collaborator."

Kitty gasped, unable to defend her, without giving this lady too much information and endangering them all. What was it Raymond said, 'there is still love in war.' Hadn't she herself, almost warmed to that German who helped her into the hospital? Was it ever as clear cut as good and bad? Good people are capable of doing terrible things, and vice versa. What should she say now?

"Thank you, Madame. I appreciate your kindness in warning me. My aunty has been foolish, and I do not want a part of that. Those beasts killed my husband, how could she engage with them like that?"

Madame Thomas stroked her arm. "Whoever you are, wherever you are from, bon chance. Now you must leave here, and please do not ever give anyone the

KITTY TAYLOR by Sarah Colliver

impression that I am anything but a cantankerous and nosy neighbour. I have a reputation to uphold."

Kitty smiled. "Merci, au revoir." Her head reeled as she crept back to the shop. The lady whom she felt a threat was not, and the person she felt safe with, who had lived with and taken for granted as trustworthy, had been seeing a German officer all along. A German who had kept them in cigarettes, and had given them a mountain of onions, which were probably from a poor innocent French farmer. She felt sick. How would she face her? Should she confront her?

She closed the shop door behind her. And crept back up the stairs, where Valerie was now making coffee in the kitchen.

"What were you doing in her house? That woman is dangerous with her sharp tongue."

"Her cat, I was taking it back to her as it found its way into our courtyard, and she was calling it." Kitty hoped she sounded convincing.

"Ahh, I see. Coffee?"

KITTY TAYLOR by Sarah Colliver

"Merci." Kitty sank onto the chair, and felt as though the world was collapsing around her."

"You look dreadful, no sleep I guess?"

"No. Watched the clock all night. We must talk; please will you sit down." Kitty took a deep breath and pulled out the chair beside her.

"Of course. What is it, Cherie?"

"Well, I'm leaving today. I can't tell you where I'm going, but I'm leaving the area."

"Today? Why so sudden?" Valerie's brow furrowed.

"Oh, it's not sudden to me, but I can only say what really needs to be said, you understand."

Valerie's eyes pooled with tears. "I shall miss you so much. It's been wonderful to have your company. Will you be okay? Have you anywhere safe to go?"

"I really can't say anything else. You know that."

Valerie nodded and wiped her face with her hanky.

Kitty wanted Valerie to know that her secret was out, that she knew about the German officer, and

KITTY TAYLOR by Sarah Colliver

pondered whether this was the right thing to do. Would it be best to pretend everything was ok? She wanted to scream at her and shake her. To ask her over and over, why?

"We didn't even get a chance to sort out the courtyard, but perhaps I can manage that on my own."

"You could ask your 'friend' to help? If I'm not here, maybe he could come over, you could even consider making it more official?" Kitty knew that she couldn't stay silent.

Valerie stood up and pulled down the cow tin, "Cigarette?"

Kitty shook her head, "Non, merci." She didn't want anything from any German.

Valerie looked surprised. "Unlike you to refuse."

"I fear it may choke me, now I understand who your 'friend' is and why discretion is needed. I understand it was your 'friend' who stepped in and saved you the other night, from the two drunks. For that I am grateful. But, how? How could you? It's bad enough that you are with a German, but to allow me to stay here, pretending I am safe?"

"But don't you see, it made you safer, why would anyone check here? One word to him, and we would be protected."

"Oh, how sad this makes me. Valerie, one wrong word to him and we would both be DEAD! I have tried to blend in, to be almost invisible, to slip under everyone's radar, and all the time you are busy drawing attention by collaborating with the enemy!"

"How dare you call me that! I have risked my life to help the war effort. I have kept you safe. I have never, ever given him any cause to be suspicious." Valerie stood and pointed her finger accusingly.

"I wonder if this, putting me up, and offering me safety, is purely to ease your conscience, to appease yourself from the fact you are sleeping with the enemy."

Valerie's slap stung, but the situation and grisly facts hurt the most. "I'm sorry, Cherie. I didn't mean to hurt you, but you made me so mad."

KITTY TAYLOR by Sarah Colliver

"Don't call me Cherie. My name is Giselle." Kitty stood and grabbed her bag from the hook.

"Bon chance Valerie. You are going to need all the luck you can get, because people don't take kindly to women getting in to bed with the enemy. And I am afraid that is all they will see."

"Wait! I want you to know that I didn't do this to appease any guilt, I did it genuinely to help. And I am so fond of you, your parents should be proud of their daughter. Trouble is, you can't help who you fall for. He isn't like the others, he's kind and wants this war to end, the same as we do. He doesn't want to hurt anyone, but he must follow his orders or they will shoot him, don't you see? Aren't we all simply people at the end of the day?"

"I watched an execution, not long after I arrived here. One man, beaten to a pulp, marched into a quaint little square, which had been teeming with everyday life moments before. Twenty men marched that man into the square. He could barely walk. They gathered us all, rounded us up into a macabre audience for their performance. The officer didn't get his own hands dirty, he simply nodded at a subordinate whom without flinching, stepped forward and pulled the trigger. That man's final word, from his hoarse throat, was 'Liberte.' I don't think I need to say another word, but if that story doesn't remind you of who *you* are, and what *they* represent, then you are as bad as them, Valerie. Don't think, not for one second, that if it came down to it and he was given the order to shoot you in a square surrounded by horrified eyes, that he would disobey that order. Is that love?"

Kitty turned away, her eyes burning. She felt such a wave of grief, that a person she had trusted and become so fond of, had tricked her. This time in France, had taught her so much about other people, and their ability to pray on trust. She closed the shop door for a final time and sighed. As she walked up the street, Madame Thomas waved from her window. Once Kitty turned the corner, she slumped against a wall, which was graffitied with 'Fuck the Germans' and thought how appropriate this was, considering what she had recently discovered about Valerie. She checked all around and pushed away the fear of being caught with her weapon on the way to the barn. The longest route would be safest. Her luck seemed to be wearing thin, and she did not want to tempt fate.

KITTY TAYLOR by Sarah Colliver

As she trod the streets which had become so familiar, her heavy heart reminded her that she was saying goodbye. Her heart ached for Valerie, who would be condemned to a brutal end by her compatriots. She made Kitty feel welcome and loved. With so much kindness and love to offer, Kitty could not understand why it had to be given to a German, instead of one of her French admirers she talked about. It reminded her that humans are capable of both good and bad, that love can blind people to reality, and it hit home, how close she had come to allowing Sebastian to cloud her mind. It felt like an eternity since their sweet romance back home, when she longed for his touch. Now she saw him for what he was. A Lothario, who only cared for himself and satisfying his own needs. It must have been easy for him, to hide behind the whole, 'I can't talk about it because of my job,' line. How many young women did he have stringing along behind him? She shrugged away the dirty feeling these thoughts gave her.

When she arrived at the edge of town, near the café where poor Henri had been arrested, she dropped to tie up her shoelace, and stall for long enough to take a last look at the town. As she stood, she crossed her fingers that she would come back there to visit, in peace time, when the Germans had been chased back to their own country. She turned and headed for the familiar woodland path.

She slumped down on a mound of soft green moss and took a moment to breathe and think. If all went to plan, she would soon be leaving France behind. Her beloved country, which was currently stained with all the bloodshed caused by the Nazis. Her broken fingers were black and blue, and her mind full of information which would be useful during de-brief. It was a bitter-sweet moment, saying goodbye to France, but she knew that a break was needed for her to work effectively. Perhaps they would send her back again after a rest? It didn't feel as though the end of the war was imminent yet, so they would still be needing people like her.

She lay back and stared up between the towering trees, to the blue sky. The clouds were fast moving, and she inhaled the sweet pine scent. In that moment, it was hard to believe there was a world war being fought. The forest felt protective, like a natural fortress, especially the deeper you went. It was as though the magical trees cast spells of disorientation and created

KITTY TAYLOR by Sarah Colliver

a shielding camouflage. But it was important to remember that machine guns and fire, could penetrate their safety, and as ever, it was imperative not to draw attention that way. Was anywhere truly safe these days?

A memory stole her away to the safety of home, where her mother was busy putting together a tray of tea and scolding her for being late home. It was no wonder she was so against Kitty going into uniform when her mother had been so actively involved in the last war: stitching up flesh, holding the hands of those on the edge of life. Her mother had every right to behave so protectively. Kitty longed for a chance to tell her so. A bird swooped from above and, without stopping, swiped a tiny mouse from the ground. A predator hiding among the thicket...

The barn was silent, and Kitty was unsure if that was a good or bad sign. She remembered her mother's old saying, that you should only worry about children when they go quiet. Was it the same in this situation? What if Sebastian were in deeper than she thought, he could have given away the barn location... The hair on her neck prickled and she shuddered, suddenly chilly.

KITTY TAYLOR by Sarah Colliver

The ground under foot was uneven with roots and rocks, so she carefully tiptoed along the edge of the treeline, and around the back to see if she could hear anything. The back of the barn was entirely stone with two tiny open windows. Decrepit carts and crates lay abandoned and unloved, with grass growing up through them like a parasite. The barn was Raymond's father's, and they used to keep animals there. It must have been teeming with life back then. Checking to make sure no one was around, she tiptoed to the wall and listened. Was that movement she could hear- a rustling of hay? Her stomach lurched. Perhaps she should run.

She quietly climbed onto the rickety cart and peered into the small window opening. Raymond and Lucile, were slumped on the floor, both gagged and tied to separate, ancient barn posts. And Sebastian, sat facing the door, a gun in his hand. Was he waiting for her? The radio sat on the table which usually held Raymond's maps and wine glass. What was his plan? Perhaps she should shoot him in the back of the head... a movement to the right caught her eye. A lady sidled up to him, kissed him passionately and then whispered in his ear. Kitty could not hear what she said. Sebastian reached up and cupped her breasts, there was a familiarity between them, an ease. There was no time for the regret, disgust, and frustration which crept up when thinking about all the times she allowed him to touch her. Their intimate, shared moments were all lies. He must have mocked how easy she was to sweet talk into bed. Her cheeks flushed with rage. What was he up to? Suddenly the mist in her mind cleared. She knew. He *was* the informant, a double agent. For how long, she didn't know, but London had no idea, they were intent on getting him back to safety. He had been tailing Philippe, was responsible for Henri's arrest. Did he bring down the other circuit rather than escaping it? Strange that he appeared as she was about to meet with Henri, had he planned for her arrest too? Her blood ran cold, she was in more danger than she thought. The Gestapo could be on the way. She shivered and fought to regain control of the panic which threatened to manifest a scream. Kitty silently climbed down and pushed her back flat against the wall as she rooted in her bag for her hidden revolver.

She looked again at Lucile and Raymond. They were not moving at all. Were they dead? There didn't appear to be any blood stains. Her mind swirled with information, and she knew there was only a few moments to address the whole messy situation. This could be the end for her. She would never get to see her home again, never sit at a noisy family dinner where everyone talks over each other, or hold Grand-mère's hand.

She pushed the revolver into the belt of her trousers, pulled her cardigan over it, and slung her bag over her shoulder as she crept back to the trees for a moment. Perhaps she should fake her arrival, as though she was unaware of what lay in wait...she had the upper hand after all, now she knew the situation inside the barn. Sebastian and his floozy would be unaware that she had seen them, or had any idea of the evolving situation.

Kitty took a deep breath, and with every ounce of courage she could find, wandered towards the barn door. Before she could think any more, she pushed through it.

"Michel? What's going on? What's happened?" Kitty turned to Lucile and Raymond. "Are they okay? I don't understand!" Kitty hoped her voice was more convincing than it sounded to herself.

KITTY TAYLOR by Sarah Colliver

Sebastian stood and slowly walked towards her; his eyes fixed on her face. He clutched his revolver, but his arm hung by his side. Kitty edged backwards until she pressed against the door. An image of the brave man murdered in the square- his bound hands behind him, clutching the tree- sprung to mind. "Are you okay? You look…I don't know…"

"My Kitty. I've been waiting for you." He pushed his body against her and forced his lips onto hers. She froze. What was he doing? He grabbed her arm and twisted it up behind her back, her face pressed against the rough old wood of the door. She prayed he would not feel her gun.

"I don't understand. What is this?" She spoke in a low controlled voice despite her fear.

He yanked her twisted arm and pushed her onto the chair where he had sat awaiting her arrival. Then he stepped backwards.

"Hello Kitty, sorry, Giselle. I mean which would you prefer?" It was a perfect British accent, and she spoke in English.

KITTY TAYLOR by Sarah Colliver

Kitty looked to her left where the woman stood leaning on a ladder to the hayloft, her arms folded. She had jet black hair and looked out of place in such a rural setting, with her perfectly tailored trousers and blouse.

"Je suis Giselle," Kitty responded defiantly, holding her steely stare.

"Save your lies. It's all too late for that. Michel has told me all about you. Don't worry about your friends, they aren't dead, they're far too valuable."

Sebastian watched the scene from a distance, and Kitty realised that he wasn't in charge here. It was the woman. "What do you want with me?"

"Where and when is the next drop? We know it's soon. That's why you're here, why you told Michel to stay put."

"You know I will never tell you that." Kitty meant it. She would go out fighting and was grateful that they hadn't bound her, that she could still reach her gun. Trouble was they were both armed, and if she shot one of them, the other would shoot her. She couldn't risk being captured alive. She would need to bide her time. "You haven't introduced yourself, at least allow me to know who is holding me captive."

"You can call me Philomene, Michel's fiancé."

"His fiancé? Since when?"

"Oh, don't worry about all *that*. I know all about your little frisson. Purely business, anything goes in these dark days of war. And I can't blame you, he really is difficult to turn down." Philomene gazed towards Sebastian and licked her lips. Kitty's stomach turned over; he had never looked less appealing. He stood awkwardly and anything which may have attracted her once had dissipated. All she saw now was a double-crossing, creepy man.

"So, where were we. Ah yes, the radio." Philomene switched it on. "Now, what was the message we are waiting for?"

Kitty glared at Sebastian, who skilfully avoided her eyes. The strange, coded messages began to play, "The boat sits high in the water. Three stars are out to shine…"

KITTY TAYLOR by Sarah Colliver

"So, we wait. And perhaps, you might be persuaded to tell me more…" She crouched beside Lucile, and pointed the gun to her head. "Now."

"Leave her alone!" Kitty yelled.

"You can save her, if you tell me when and where." Philomene gently moved a lock of Lucile's hair from her forehead. "I will let her go. Come on, talk to me. Tell us what we need to know,"

"She's pregnant, please don't hurt her any more than you have already." Kitty knew she was clutching at straws.

"One more French bastard child! That won't affect the outcome here, do you think the Gestapo will take pity on her because of that?" Philomene laughed.

Kitty's mind whirred. Poor Lucile.

"Okay, please stop pointing the gun at her. I will tell you." Kitty was listening out for her message amongst the nonsensical phrases churning out of the radio.

Philomene stood up and pointed her gun towards Kitty. "Like I said, they are worth more alive. And now, we can use her unborn child as leverage, so that is already a useful snippet. Thank you."

Kitty flushed with anger. She wanted to tear at her face and scream, but instead controlled her voice and spoke quietly, "So far, the go ahead hasn't come through..."

"Liar." Philomene's face scowled.

"It's true. I've been listening out for it." Kitty wasn't lying.

Philomene crouched in front of Kitty, and grabbed her chin between her fingers, pushing her face from side to side. "I can see why you enjoyed her so much; she is pretty enough." She laughed.

Kitty fought the urge to smack her hand away. She must remain untethered if she was to have any chance of surviving, and that meant holding back and toeing the line, for now.

Sebastian smiled. "We had our moments, didn't we?"

Kitty stared at the ground, unable to voice the words she wished to launch. How was she going to get them out of this? She looked to Sebastian and thought maybe he was her way out. Surely he must feel something for her, so she held his gaze, but his eyes were empty.

"Oh, how sweet. She thinks you might help her out of this little quandary..." Philomene's patronising tone mocked Kitty.

The radio continued, and as the clipped British accent confirmed their code, Kitty fought to keep any recognition from appearing on her face. The messages ended, and Philomene pulled Kitty to her feet. "Now, you are going to tell me, have you heard the message, when is the drop and where?"

"I didn't hear the go ahead and I would never tell you anything."

Philomene's blow sent Kitty flying to the floor. Her head reeled and she landed on her injured fingers, which sent shooting pains up her arm. She refused her scream, unwilling to satisfy this sadist.

"So, you want to play it that way?" Philomene walked over to Lucile, untied her and slapped her face. "Wakey, wakey, darling."

KITTY TAYLOR by Sarah Colliver

Kitty watched in horror as Lucile awoke with eyes filled with fear. What had gone on before her arrival?

"Come and sit on this chair... Come on." She yanked Lucile from the ground and pushed her onto the chair. "Look Lucile, we have a visitor, and she has told me all about you. I hear congratulations are in order."

Kitty's gathering rage drowned her pain, and she looked towards Raymond. He wasn't unconscious, he was only pretending. Sebastian watched Philomene but said nothing.

"You need to tell me all about the drop, save your little baby..."

"I wasn't told anything. I told you before," Lucile whimpered.

"Liar!" Philomene yanked her head back by her hair until she faced the roof. "Do you know what the Gestapo will do to your foetus?" She licked her lips and then whispered into Lucile's ear. The colour drained from her face. Lucile's eyes pooled with tears and her lips quivered.

KITTY TAYLOR by Sarah Colliver

Kitty turned her head towards Sebastian. "Why are you doing this Sebastian? I thought you loved me, you always came and found me in London. We were good together, weren't we? You were the only man I could have ever loved."

Sebastian jolted and looked towards Kitty with softened eyes, as though she had stirred memories he had long shut out.

"Don't speak until I tell you to, unless you want me to kill this one and her foetus?" Philomene pointed to Lucile's stomach with her pistol.

"Oh, now that's brave, you must feel powerful, picking on a defenceless pregnant woman," Kitty shouted and began to stand.

"Shut up! How dare you speak to me like that." Philomene ran at Kitty and kicked her back to the floor. Kitty curled into a defensive ball as the blows continued. Still, she refused to make a sound. It was pure rage that kept her blood rushing and stopped the pain from crippling her.

"So, Michel, London? Forgot to mention that little detail, thought it was purely a France thing."

KITTY TAYLOR by Sarah Colliver

Philomene sidled up to him and brushed her gun against his cheek.

Kitty took the opportunity to silently check in on Lucile who was shivering, her body clearly going into shock with everything that was happening. Raymond was slowly undoing his bound hands, making only the slightest, unnoticeable movement. Was Philomene about to turn on Sebastian?

"It meant nothing, she was one of many. I was socked when she turned up unexpectedly." Sebastian brushed his lips over hers. "There's only one woman for me. You know that. I don't see anyone else, only you."

Philomene allowed his kiss, but as she pulled away, she bit his lip, enough to draw a little blood, show him who was in charge. "This was the one who you had me hide downstairs for. Who visited our little love den, uninvited, and silly you pretended to search for the back door keys when she suggested leaving out of the back?"

Kitty's eyes widened as she remembered the scene. At the time, she was uneasy when he made such a fuss about finding his keys to the backdoor. And now she knew - Philomene was hiding there. That was why he stalled her, encouraged her to leave from the front. Her instinct had been spot on! She must learn to listen to it, trust and be guided by it. Perhaps if she had found out then, this situation would never have happened.

Sebastian nodded. Was that a look of shame on his face? If it wasn't, it should be. Shame should be coursing through his veins. For betraying his country, and his comrades. For what- this bitch to order him around? None of this made any sense. Could he really be that blinded by his desire?

"This is getting tedious now. So, let's see what we can do about that. I have places to go, people to see and I need information. Who is going to be the one to give it to me?" Philomene swung her revolver around, pointing at each of them in turn.

Sebastian grabbed Kitty, and held down her arms, pushing the cold metal barrel into her temple, as Philomene headed towards Raymond. "Hmm, he's been very quiet over here." She kicked him, as though testing his reflexes. "You still sleeping? Oh, but you're missing all the fun!"

KITTY TAYLOR by Sarah Colliver

Kitty whispered, "Please let us go. This isn't right. This isn't who you are, Sebastian, you know me."

"Shut up," his irritated voice spat the words.

Kitty looked to Lucile, who sat squirming silently in a pool of urine, watching the chaos unfold around her, fear twisting her face.

"Raymond? Don't you want to save your unborn baby?" Philomene strode back to Lucile. "Oh! You appear to have pissed yourself darling, did you hear that, Raymond? She's wet herself- how unbecoming." Philomene laughed and pointed to the puddle on the floor.

With the force of a blast, Raymond launched himself at Philomene, and tackled her to the ground, smacking her head to the stone floor where blood immediately gushed from the wound. Lucile screamed, and Sebastian flinched and hesitated, enough for Kitty to grab her pistol. She pulled the trigger, and he fell to the floor with his eyes fixed on her, his pistol falling too. Lucile scrambled from her chair and grabbed it, turning it on Philomene. Lucile screamed from the depths of her womb as the bullets tore at Philomene's flesh.

KITTY TAYLOR by Sarah Colliver

Kitty, crouched beside Sebastian. She hadn't meant to kill, only to wound, but he was heavily bleeding. "Who knows about us? Does anyone know about Lucile and Raymond or this place? If you want to redeem yourself, you need to tell me. Are we safe?"

Sebastian drifted in and out of consciousness, and it seemed, time. He smiled at Kitty and looked like the man she had once fallen for. "You're my Kitty."

"Please, you must tell us. Are we safe here?" Kitty pleaded.

His eyes widened and fixed on Kitty. "She knew nothing about here, and your identities, until today."

Kitty sighed with relief that the Gestapo weren't enroute. That was a small mercy. "Why? What made you do this?" Kitty began ripping up a towel which was hung from a rusty hook, and applied pressure to the wound, to try and stem the bleeding.

"They don't know what it's like, coming out here, time after time. You tell so many lies, you don't know what's real anymore…"

Lucile and Raymond stood over her shoulder.

KITTY TAYLOR by Sarah Colliver

"Leave him to die. He doesn't deserve our help; do you think he would have saved us? Did he do anything to help her?" Raymond clutched Lucile into his chest protectively.

"It's too late anyway. He's lost too much blood, and I can't help him. May you find peace in your actions, Sebastian." Kitty made the sign of the cross on his forehead and stood up, trying to piece together everything that had happened. "She's dead I take it?" Kitty walked over to Philomene's lifeless body; the torn flesh stained with crimson. Kitty's legs threatened to buckle as pain began to flood her battered body. She must hold it together, in a few hours, all going to plan, she would be on the plane and could rest then. "Get his wallet and check for anything else he has."

Kitty crouched beside Philomene and searched her pockets. Nothing. "Look for a bag, anything, she must have had her ID on her."

"Over there, I remember." Lucile pointed to a coat and bag on a crate in the corner.

Kitty ran to it and pulled out the contents. She threw the cigarettes to Raymond and opened the

KITTY TAYLOR by Sarah Colliver

identification papers. She would take them back with her for London to figure out, and put it all back inside the bag, along with the items removed from Sebastian.

"We need to get this blood cleaned up, and those two buried. I know he said no one knows about this place, but I think we should find another place to wait until tonight. You will need to make sure no one is watching it before you come back... Lucile, you need hot water and fresh clothes."

"No one is home, we can go there. It's out of town anyway, just through the trees," Lucile offered.

"Right. Let's clear up and get going."

"Giselle, what was that about London, you and him." Lucile nodded her head towards Sebastian's body.

"You know I can't say too much. But let's say that when I ran into him it was a huge surprise. I had no idea that this was his job, or that we would meet this way. I knew him from home."

Raymond stared, as though processing what she had said. "You should have mentioned it, and you should have told London."

KITTY TAYLOR by Sarah Colliver

"Maybe, but I didn't know anything, only that he was out here, doing what I am. If I had suspected him, I would have reported him immediately. No, if I had thought he was a double agent, I would have made sure he was taken care of immediately. But you know that, surely?"

He paused and then nodded. "Yes, I know, but you should have told us that you knew him from before, at least."

Kitty tucked Philomene's bag into her rucksack, and inwardly acknowledged that he was right, she should have said something.

"Can I speak to you for a moment?" Raymond touched Kitty's arm and pulled her outside.

"You must take her with you tonight. I cannot do this, knowing the danger she is in. Hearing about what would happen to her and our baby if she is captured. Everything is different now. You must take her."

Kitty nodded, "I agree, but how? She will never leave you."

"Leave that to me, okay?"

KITTY TAYLOR by Sarah Colliver

TIME TO LEAVE

The rumbling engine of the plane drew nearer, and Kitty was immediately transported back to her arrival, and the fear. She half expected to be ambushed, that the German's were already alerted to them, watching them, and vomit rose from her empty stomach. The pain from earlier came in waves, depending on her stress levels. She still wasn't sure how they would manage to get Lucile on the plane, and it would stop for only moments, time was not on their side.

The lit beacons guided the plane down, and two shadowy figures emerged and ran towards them. "Dominique!"

"Giselle! You look dreadful, are you ok, can I help you?"

"I'm fine, Raymond will look after you. Bon Chance!" They briefly squeezed hands, both aware that they all needed to get away as soon as they could manage.

Raymond ran towards the plane, followed by Lucile. "Get in Lucile, now! I don't want you here. You saw what can happen to us. If you won't do it for me, do it for our baby." He sank to his knees and grabbed her waist kissing her stomach, and then pushed her away. "Now go!" He turned and ran towards Dominique, ordering them to follow him.

"Lucile, get in quickly. We must leave," Kitty shouted.

"I can't, I won't," she screamed.

"Do you want to kill us all, including this pilot who has risked his life for us?"

"No."

"Get in now." Kitty pushed Lucile up into the small seat, and jumped in behind her. The plane was already moving and within moments gaining speed and height.

Lucile's sobs deepened, and Kitty's body began to violently shake. It was as though the events of the day, and her injuries were punishing her body and sending it into shock.

"What is it? What's the matter?" Lucile shouted above the din of the engine.

"It's okay. I'll be okay. We'll be home soon enough…" Kitty whispered over and over, as her body continued to judder and her tears blinded her eyes.

KITTY TAYLOR by Sarah Colliver

DE-BRIEF

"Kitty, you look dreadful!" Sylvia sounded genuinely concerned, despite the wide smile she could not supress, that Kitty had made it home.

"My bruising's come out, that's all. Looks worse than it is," Kitty lied. The pain came from every part of her exhausted body.

"They bombed the target last night, thanks to you. They won't be making anything in that factory again."

"I know that may seem like good news, but it's easy to forget, sat here at this desk, far away, that there are innocent people, living and working alongside that building..."

"You cannot think like that, this is war Kitty. We are bombed relentlessly. The target you helped clarify would have churned out many bombs, to be used to kill our civilians, which is how you must think of it."

Kitty half smiled, she knew she was right, but it was a hard fact to digest. Perhaps after a proper rest she would manage to think differently, but it was still all too raw. "Madame Aubert, it turns out, had a German officer lover, so it's lucky I'm here at all. And what about Sebastian, Philomene?"

"Sebastian was a shocker. He was one of our best, experienced, and spent prolonged periods out there."

"He liked the ladies," Kitty offered.

"We knew about you and him, but never thought your paths should cross. Totally different areas, you see."

Kitty took a cigarette from the box on the desk, and lit it, angered that they knew. They had put her life in even more danger, but he was thought to be a good agent, not one that would pose a threat anyway. It was all so bloody complicated, like peeling layers on the onions she chopped up for her soup.

"Philomene, we had eyes on for a long time, but we lost her. She would work on the men, lure them into bed to get any information she could, then turn them in, for the Gestapo to extract the rest. She too, was from the North and the last person we expected to turn up in your area. There was a planned assassination, guess who we sent to do that?"

Kitty gasped, "Sebastian?"

KITTY TAYLOR by Sarah Colliver

"We should have known he wouldn't be able to resist her. When he disappeared, we feared the worst, that he was yet another victim of hers. It seems he got hold of an identity we knew nothing of, and headed to your circuit, to infiltrate it. So, this outcome really is more than we could have hoped. I know you don't want to hear it but well done."

"It's not appropriate, I haven't baked a lovely cake or won a race. How's Lucile? I was worried about her. You know she's pregnant?"

"She is being de-briefed too and will then be on bed rest no doubt. You did the right thing bringing her back. She would have been a liability out there."

"When can I go home? I want to see my family." Kitty felt the sudden need to be enveloped by warmth and love, the things she would have considered as irritating and stifling before.

"Once we have completed the debrief, which we must begin now, but one thing before we do: Kitty, I must tell you, I have bad news."

Kitty's heart sank, and tears stung her tired eyes. "Grand-mère."

KITTY TAYLOR by Sarah Colliver

"Yes, I'm afraid she passed a few days after you left. But that's not what I was going to say."

Kitty's throat constricted, and she felt as though she was gasping for air like a fish out of water.

"I'm afraid your mother was killed, the communal shelter she took refuge in on her way home from work, suffered a direct hit."

"My mother?" Kitty felt the blood drain from her body, and she shook.

Sylvia stood and poured them both a brandy. She put the glass to Kitty's lips. "Sip this, for the shock. I'm so sorry."

Kitty's mind threw out every mean word she had spoken to her mother, which then attacked and pecked at her conscience. What was the last thing she said to her? How had they parted? It felt so long ago. "When?"

"Last week. The funeral is in a couple of days. I have this too, it's your letters, sent to you whilst you were out in France."

"Thank you, it's her handwriting. My mother's."

KITTY TAYLOR by Sarah Colliver

"Here, please take this." Sylvia handed over a lace-edged handkerchief.

Kitty sobbed, aware that she still had the official debrief to get through, but with a desperation to read her mother's final words. She sipped the brandy and pulled herself together for one last push. Then she would be allowed home, armed with her cover story as to why she was battered and bruised.

HELLO, GOODDBYE

Kitty stared through her tears, nothing felt real. Since returning from France, life was a whirlwind of uncertainties. She sucked in her stomach and smoothed her skirt, feeling proud in her uniform. Despite the fact her mother did not initially approve, the letter Kitty received on returning from France, brought real comfort as her mother had written words of pride and love. Kitty wished she could have read the letter at the time it was sent and been able to reply. But it was a month old, and too late now. Her mother

KITTY TAYLOR by Sarah Colliver

would never know how grateful she was to receive her kind words.

Kitty glanced to the left, where Grand- mère's recent grave lay, still a mound of earth, and finally allowed the heavy tears to fall. They fell for both women, who now lay dead before her. She cried for herself too, how it had taken a brutal mission in an occupied country, to learn about people, their motives, and to understand that maybe she could build a relationship with her mother. But it was all too late. Kitty blew a kiss towards each of the women, and wiped her nose, wondering how she would navigate through this loss.

Anna walked carefully around the gravesite and stood next to Kitty. She rubbed Kitty's back; her red eyes full of concern for her sister. Everyone else from the funeral party had gone, only the grave diggers lurked, waiting to complete their job and fill in the hole, where her mother was lowered only minutes before. "I have so much I wanted to say to her Anna, and now I'll never get the chance."

"She left something, for *you*. When we get back, I'll give it to you, it's a letter."

KITTY TAYLOR by Sarah Colliver

"I got the letter when I arrived back." Kitty realised her error and hoped Anna was too emotional to question her, "I mean we got given mail regularly, only we couldn't always reply, working around the clock you know?"

"No, not that one. She left this one on the side, ready to post. Never got the chance." Anna's face twisted with tears, and she buried her head in Kitty's shoulder.

Kitty pulled Anna in tight and sniffed. "I hope you aren't getting your make up on my uniform!" She attempted to lighten the moment for them both then turned her attention towards the two men leaning on their shovels, smoking a cigarette. She wanted to berate them for being disrespectful, ask them what they were waiting for, and didn't they know it was rude to stare? But she didn't have the energy. "Come on, let's get a drink, I could do with a large one."

"Where's your luggage? We were hoping you would get home in time for today, but it's a shame we couldn't have seen you before the funeral."

KITTY TAYLOR by Sarah Colliver

"Only barely made it, there were delays on the trains. I didn't think I was going to make it, the taxi driver took pity on me and agreed to drop my luggage at the hall."

Anna linked arms with Kitty, "I'm so glad you made it back, it's not the same without you, and the house feels so empty. Dad doesn't even speak on the rare occasion he is home. He only comes home to eat and then goes back out again. Either working or on duty with the Home Guard. Sophie is spending more time at Sid's mum's house. She lost her other son last month when his plane was shot down. Sophie started off being her rock, but I suppose it works both ways now Mum's gone."

"What a time this is to live. I sort of understand what Mother was talking about now, about how scarred she was from the last war. We will all be left with them too, from this one." She wished she could have that conversation again, tell her that she understood. "Well, I'm here, for now at least."

"It's been dreadful, so many from around here lost. It feels so dark and oppressive...like the sun no longer shines. The little coffins, they are the ones that get me most."

KITTY TAYLOR by Sarah Colliver

The sisters followed the stony path away from the graveside, passed two other gatherings of mourners. Death was big business in these dark days of war.

"Manon is meeting us at the hall, she was desperate to see you."

"How is she?" Kitty knew she would fall apart in her arms.

"She is shutting up early to come to the wake. She looks tired, and misses you, we all do."

"Is that my brooch Anna?" Kitty smiled; some things never changed.

"I got it from Sophie, she said I could have it." Anna gently pressed her fingers into the pasted jewelled rose, as though it were worth millions.

"Well, it wasn't hers to give but, keep it, it looks lovely on you." Kitty kissed Anna's cheek, and they strode away from the church yard and towards the Victoria Hall, where they would raise a glass to the two ladies. Kitty thought about the last time she went to the hall, dancing with her sisters. There would be no chance of Sebastian turning up this time. There was so much she still had to hide, and couldn't say, so she would be careful not to loosen her tongue by drinking too much. Secrets and lies had become a necessity of her survival now, and she wondered if there would ever be a time when she could live a normal life again.

Kitty was drifting off into a comfortable and slightly boozy slumber when she remembered the letter. The day had taken its toll, and the feeling of laying in her own familiar bed, at the in-between state of awake and sleep, almost caused her to forget that her mother was gone. Anna was right, the house felt empty. They were used to their mother pouncing on them before they had managed to get in through the door, with her offerings of tea, or questions about their day. Now, it was silent, and no pot of tea sat warming.

Kitty sighed and sat up, her mind whirled with thoughts. Was Raymond alive? Had Valerie been found out? How she had misjudged Madame Thomas. Why did Sebastian turn? But she pushed them all aside, that was Giselle. Today she was Kitty. It was a surprise that seeing Grand-mère's bedroom back as the dining room was a relief. The old lady would have been angry about laying there day after day, waiting for death to come. This brought Kitty more peace than seeing her enduring a state of living death. She had begun to grieve for her long ago. Her mother, that was the shock: all those years wasted at odds. She staggered out of bed and down to the mantle over the fire, where the letter was propped up against the clock, which ticked loudly.

Sinking into the armchair, where her mother spent many hours darning, sewing, and chatting with anyone who visited, Kitty pressed the envelope to her lips. The familiar cursive lettering from her mother's neat handwriting brought a smile to her face. This really was a gift. She would savour these final, written words.

KITTY TAYLOR by Sarah Colliver

My dearest Kitty,

I don't know if this letter will make it to you intact, or be heavily censored, but I hope you will at least understand what I am trying to say to you.

I have given this much thought and am grateful to have this opportunity to write down my words, which I hope will bring you comfort and affirmation that you are loved.

We haven't always seen eye to eye, have we? I think that is a common theme with some mothers and daughters, but I know I have been a source of irritation to you, and losing my own mother has caused me to reflect on many things. Not least, you and I.

You have always been drawn towards my mother, and she to you. As though you shared a special bond, and it

KITTY TAYLOR by Sarah Colliver

happened straight away, always extra smiles for Grand-mère!

What you must know is that Dad and I both felt blessed when we found out about you. Remember the war and death we had both been immersed in? Well, you were our reason to fight our way back to life and offered me a fresh start, away from the landscape of death. England gave me hope, a chance to leave behind the war, although the images, sadly, haunt me to this day.

We were excited to build a home together and bring life into the world, our little Katarina, despite the whisperings about us.

I was so determined to settle in and create a home, to improve my English and make new traditions, I fear I pushed you away, when all you wanted to do was embrace your French heritage. But my lovely Kitty, I am so proud of you, of all you have learned and absorbed from your Grand-mère, for staying true to who you are.

I have been dreaming about you. You are always in France, and you are in danger. It is the same dream, night after night. I know I got a letter from you, from Scotland, which I have already replied to, but I am your mother, and I don't think you are in Scotland, or that you will even see this letter until you return from where you really are. That is why I shall not receive a reply from you, because you cannot read my words until you return home.

Kitty, I want to tell you, that I am so proud of you. Of all you stand for. Of your courage, and determination. Proud that you are MY daughter, and came from the love your dad and I share.

When you return home, I truly hope we can both be more honest and loving. I know how much you will struggle without your Grand-mère, but you should know her passing was peaceful. And I don't believe she would ever leave you. I feel she is wherever you are now, protecting you, and that brings me much comfort.

Come home safe,,

Your loving mother

Xxx

KITTY TAYLOR by Sarah Colliver

Kitty sobbed. Everything she could have wished for was in those written words. The irony was that if the letter had ever been sent, it would have been heavily censored, if delivered at all from the tone of it. Her mother knew. She gave her blessing. She loved her. And now, Kitty was armed with what she needed to carry on. This leave offered her time to grieve, to process, and to rest, before Baker Street would call, and the pull of France once again would prove too strong to ignore.

THE END, for now.

KITTY TAYLOR by Sarah Colliver

Acknowledgements

A huge THANK YOU to **Beth Matthews,** who has been so helpful with editing and offering honest feedback. You are a star!

With thanks to my Steve, James & George for championing me. Special thanks to Beth & Monika, the best DILs I could ask for, who always encourage my writing.

Thanks to my lovely friends who always make me feel worthy and help me to chase away the self-doubt.

To my readers,

Without you my stories would remain as closed books. Thank you for your support and the love you show my characters xxx

If you have enjoyed this book, please consider leaving a review on Amazon. You do not need to have bought the book on there to leave one. x

KITTY TAYLOR by Sarah Colliver

Little secrets:

I gave Kitty the name **TAYLOR**, after a young man who meant so much to our family. He will always remain in my heart.

Kitty Lives at **7 Gloster Road**, which was where my childhood home was.

Raymond was given the name because it is my maiden name.

Printed in Dunstable, United Kingdom